Haunting The Carolina Coast

Thirteen Chilling Tales Along
The Outer Banks

Joe Sledge

Cover design by Barb Noel

ISBN-978-0-9980968-9-6

First paperback edition 2022

Published by Gravity Well Books

Haunting The Carolina Coast

Thirteen Chilling Tales Along
The Outer Banks

Joe Sledge

Books by Joe Sledge

Did You See That? A Travel Guide To North Carolina's Out
Of The Ordinary Attractions

Did You See That? On The Outer Banks

Did You See That? Too!

Did You See That Ghost?

Haunting The Outer Banks

In The Shadows Of The Pines

Bess Truly And Her Zap-Gun Rangers

The Unmerciful Sea (as John Martell)

Nag's Head: Or, Two Months Among The Bankers (editor,
author of appendixes)

For Callie and Michelle

Table Of Contents

Introduction

There is a ghost in every shadow of every house, behind every tree of every graveyard on the Outer Banks. The nickname of this coast and the island chain is The Graveyard Of The Atlantic. It is a name that fits well. Thousands of shipwrecks and sinkings have occurred along our narrow coast with untold numbers of lives lost, castaways stranded, and families forever separated. Those that lost their lives at sea  but their bodies still found their way to land were often buried where they lay, and because of that the Atlantic was not the only graveyard on our coast. Cemeteries, graveyards, and even just a shallow hole or a dusting of sand might define the last resting place of a soul lost somewhere on the coast. Between the naturally wild areas and locations overgrown and hidden by time, it is likely that there are places here where no person in modern times has ever trod upon the sandy soil.

But the ghosts must be everywhere.

When I started collecting the stories for this book, I thought that it would be easy to find a new set of thirteen tales to share with my readers. There were ghost tales all around. Everyone had one. Everyone had seen a ghost at their beach house or strange lights in the trees. Surely there were more stories out there than I could ever use. Like I said, the ghosts were everywhere.

When I wrote *Haunting The Outer Banks*, I wanted to share the tales we all knew growing up on the coast, but in a new light. I wanted the stories to be told and envisioned in a different way. What I wanted was for you, dear reader, to hear them the way I did as a kid, sitting on the front porch on a summer evening, attentive and rapt with the story. We were both terrified and delighted.

What I found when writing *Haunting The Carolina Coast* was that there were a lot of these tales that were personal to us. They were really personal, unique to the teller. I found lots of stories of people staying in the old homes of the Unpainted Aristocracy, where they saw black shadows in doorways. A spectral sea captain still haunts one of them. Other figures are more vague. The pine forests of the barrier islands, or the twisted hardwoods on Roanoke Island are full of spooky apparitions that people recounted seeing as kids. The ghosts of dutiful ancestors walk old buildings from Corolla to Ocracoke, with their tap tap tap sounds and invisible presence sensed by some descendants, vehemently denied by others.

I have no doubt that, while I cannot determine if these hauntings are factual, the tales are all true to the tellers.

The difficulty I found was that the stories, like I said, while very personal to the person who experienced them, did almost nothing to lend themselves to storytelling. I could hardly share a story about how someone saw a ghost in the kitchen of their old house, and that be the end of the tale. These needed to be ghost *stories*..

The best part of an old tale told in the dying twilight of summer, while rocking chairs creak on a porch, or a fire crackles on the beach, is how it engages us into the tale. We do more than listen. We engage with the teller. We get to be part of the experience. We allow ourselves to be scared.

I found it hard to gather thirteen stories that lend themselves to storytelling, but the hard work is the reward to the reader. These stories will do more than give you a good scare, even though that is my end goal. Some are enlightening to the history of the coast and its people. I've said before that the people of the Outer Banks meet their ghosts with more fortitude than most. They open their doors a little to let the tales be part of their lives, all the while keeping a healthy respect for the ghosts that linger just in the shadows. I encourage all of us to continue that attitude. Open the book and let the tales in. Then pass them on to others. It's more fun to be scared together.

Joe Sledge

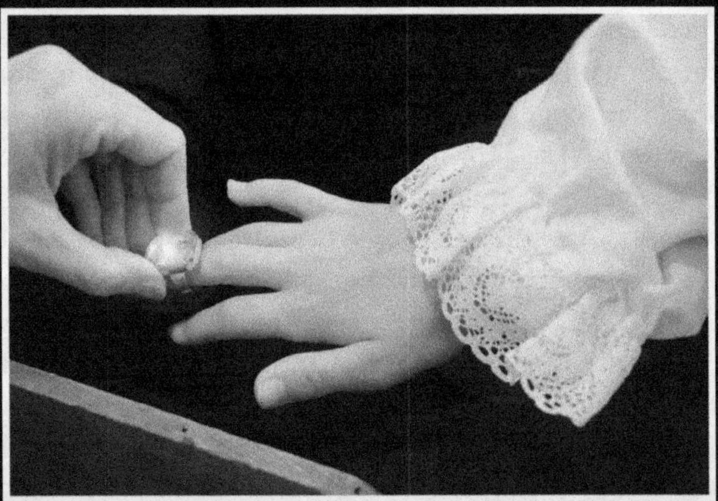

The Ring
Avon

The village of Avon has a very powerful reputation for such a small coastal town. Situated on the raw barren coast of Hatteras Island, the natives to Avon have always been strong willed and hardworking at any goal to which they set themselves. They are suspicious of outsiders and jealous of their secrets, with good reason. Preserving those secrets means preserving their way of life. They have learned from long ago to be protective of their own. Locals still refer to their home and themselves by the original name of the area, Kinnakeet.

One thing said about the people of Avon is that the women are the most beautiful that anyone ever lay eyes upon.

Local men would become extremely defensive if an outsider tried to court a Kinnakeet girl. As such, making a match on the island was a challenge. Occasionally a local man of means would be found, strong, handsome, and if not wealthy, at least secure. The difficulty might then just lie in to whom the man would be betrothed.

Such was the sad case of two sisters, orphaned when they were young and raised by neighbors to their family, with the care of the community as well. Kinnakeeters were always passionate about taking care of their own. Katharine and Margaret Gray, older and younger sisters, seemed to have a comfortable life, as much as could be for two girls who had lost their parents when they were young. Katherine, mature, more severe and worn from the life of being the older sister and the responsible one, was expected to marry before her younger sister Margaret, who was quiet and delicate, a beautiful flower of a girl who grew like a winter rose in the salt shores of Avon. That was the goal. Their adoptive father worried that the girls would grow old without the care of a husband to help provide for each of them. He arranged to meet with a handsome man named David, who made his life by the sea. David was well known for his bravery in helping others on the dangerous Atlantic Ocean as much as for his relative wealth and good looks. The father's goal was hopefully to marry the older Kate, and the attractive younger Margaret would easily attract any number of suitors.

Unfortunately for him, and ultimately for all, David would become enamoured with Margaret instead.
He visited the family several times, and ultimately professed

his love for Margaret, who reciprocated his love back wholeheartedly. Their father, worried that he would wait until his death only to see the two girls grow old as spinsters instead of Katherine ever being wed, quickly acquiesced.

David proposed, and Margaret accepted. David then presented her with a rarity hardly seen on the islands. A sparkling diamond in a silver ring, large, clear and perfect, glinted in the Outer Banks sun. It seemed to find light on the cloudiest of days, and burned like a warm fire in the sunlight. Margaret said she could feel her heart warm by the mere presence of the ring. Katherine was not warmed by it.

She burned instead.

Katherine realized she may never find a husband. She grew jealous of her sister whom she had once shared her life, the good and bad together. David the handsome surfman was supposed to be her husband, not Margaret's. And that ring that sparkled and blinded her with its light, a prideful show, should have been on her finger, not Margaret's.

So Margaret, the younger flower, was happy every day, while Katherine, the older sea oat, was sharpened by her own hate and contempt. Margaret knew when she looked at her ring as it sparkled that David's love for her would never die as long as she wore it. Even when David went out to sea Margaret was comforted by the glimmering presence of its light. She made the point to show it off and watch the light dazzle her eyes. Katherine's eyes filled with only a red fire.

One of the sad things in life along the Outer Banks back in the olden days was that people rarely lived to an old age. With little in the way of medical treatment, disease and injury took their toll. That is, when the raging Atlantic didn't take what was owed it first.

One day, David went out into a blinding storm. A ship was foundering on the shoals offshore. The people on board were in dire need of rescue. If the lifesaving boats didn't get to them, they stood no chance against the mighty waves of the sea. The lifesavers were able to get to the ship and rescue the crew and passengers, but not without a cost. In his act of bravery, David paid the ultimate sacrifice.

Margaret was brokenhearted in her loss and grief. Her love, the brightness of her life had been taken from her. She existed in a kind of stupor. Islanders noticed how she had changed from a bright flower forever in new bloom to a bud frozen in winter. Her life emptied out into a cold and noticeable decline. Only when she stared into the diamond on her hand did Margaret regain her warmth and health. If she remembered the love that her lost husband had for her, Margaret would return to her beautiful self, if only for a time. Her sister could barely hide her own shameful pride. Katherine occasionally would ask where was the fire from her ring, now that Margaret's husband was gone. Katherine became the quiet torment in Margaret's life.

Over the months after David's loss at sea, Margaret became unwell. She had slowly lost the will to go on, and was only brightened by the memory of her late husband. Margaret fell ill, and everyone could tell she had not long left to live. She passed on in her sleep on a cold spring day.

When Margaret was placed in a simple wooden coffin, the best the island could provide considering the meager supplies of the time, Katherine refused to allow anyone to sit with her at the wake. Alone with the body, with only a rough wax candle to light the gloomy room, Katherine sat in wait. She could see, even by the dim yellow glow of the flame, that the diamond still sparkled with its warmth.

Katherine's heart was moved, but only from dispassion to desire. "That diamond shouldn't be buried with my sister," she thought. "It should have been mine to begin with." With that, she reached into the open coffin and began to pull the ring off her dead sister's finger.

The ring at first would not budge. It was bonded to Margaret's hand. Katherine became upset and began to pull harder, twisting the dead girl's finger to make the ring slide off. Katherine was committed to the horrid act of grave robbing her recently deceased sister. She now fought and gave no quarter to the dead body as she twisted and broke the bones and skin before finally prying off the ring.

Katherine placed it on her own finger with a devilish smile.

At the funeral, the rest of the community gathered to pay their last respects to the sweet and quiet girl who lost too much too soon. While others grieved, Katherine cried and sniffed, using every opportunity she had to show off the sparkling diamond on her hand as she dabbed her eyes.

The people of Kinnakeet, like all the islanders of the time, could not wear a shroud of loss for long. If they did not work, they did not survive. Life was a day to day occurrence, and Margaret's death was an all too obvious example of that. If not move on, they at least moved ahead, and went back to their lives. Katherine was content, now at least partially satisfied with her reward of the ring, long fought for, long desired, now possessed.

Two days passed since the burial of Margaret, and a storm blew up from the north. The cold wind bit into the cottages and small homes that dotted the village, whipping the fires within and whistling through cracks that would need to be patched. During the night, a strange sound came to Katherine's door. A knocking that was delicate, as if done by a weak person, but also insistent. Katherine listened instead of going to the door. It seemed more like a wailing or call, with someone bumping the door as if trying to open it instead of turning the knob. Katherine felt frightened by the strange visitor in the storm and went to her bedroom to hide instead of answering it.

The next night, the storm had cleared, but the wind blew cold on a bright starlit sky. Again the visitor came, trying to get inside. But Katherine was still terrified of who this might be that had no other place to go but her home. She went to bed, only to be visited by tremulous dreams of her sister.

The next morning, Katherine went to her neighbor's house to mention the strange visitor. She explained that she thought it was Margaret, the ghost of her sister, trying to get in. Her neighbor suggested that Katherine let her sister in to see what she would want. The best way to aid a ghost, her neighbor pointed out, was to find out what would help it on its way.

That evening, the night air was warmer, with gray clouds cutting through a deep starry sky. When the sound again came to the door, she opened it. There, on the step, was her sister, an ethereal form of wisp and white, there, but not there, at the same time.

"Sister," said Katherine, her throat caught at the sight of Margaret at her door, "come inside."

The ghost fairly floated across the threshold into the small room, warmed by a fire.

"What is it that you want?" asked Katherine, with a slight mock in her voice.

"What have you done to me, Katherine?" pleaded Margaret. "I am so cold. There is no warmth in me. I feel nothing but the chill of loss."

"Where are your hands?" Katherine then asked, for she saw that Margaret hid her arms behind her thin veil of a body. Margaret's beautiful skin, her smooth hands, were hidden in the mist of a gauzy spirit.

"They are still in the grave, Katherine, so cold, ... in the grave... What have you done to me?"

With that, Katherine asked her final question, her mocking tone now open, gleeful in her victory. "And where is your beautiful diamond ring?" she said, as she held up her own hand, the diamond sparkling in the light of the roaring fire.

The next morning, the neighbor, after seeing her husband off to his fishing boat, decided to see what had happened that night with Katherine. No one had seen her come outside that day. She went to Katherine's house and found the door closed but unlocked. Knocking first, then pushing the door open, she walked inside.

Katherine was still there, sitting on the floor, staring at the last embers of a now cold hearth. Only fitful traces of smoke came from the gray and black ash. Katherine just sat and stared far off through the fire, and past the far horizon, too far to see. When the neighbor asked what had happened, if her sister had come that night, she did not answer. At first, it seemed Katherine was not responding to the words. She was not hearing what her neighbor said.

Finally, the neighbor noticed that Katherine seemed to be speaking softly, not an answer, but a chant of words only said to herself or whatever demons she saw in her stare. The old lady leaned closer to hear what Katherine said. As she looked at Katherine, she was then able to see her arm. From her ring finger, stretching up her arm, it was bruised and black, the mark of a horrible wasting of the flesh. No ring adorned her finger.

The neighbor shuddered at the sight of the strange poisoned arm. Then she heard the words uttered by Katherine as she sat in the silent and empty house.

"Cold... So cold..."

The Floating Hand
Kill Devil Hills

The Wright Brothers Monument is an imposing mark upon the hill on which it stands. Climbing up the big grassy dune, the obelisk gets taller as visitors get closer. Once they arrive at the top, it looms large in the sky as they crane their heads upward. There is a stark oversized grandeur to the giant wing shaped pylon that commemorates the Wrights' accomplishment of freeing humans from the bonds of the earth.

At the base of the pylon are two polished doors, with sets of intricate details that depict both the achievements and folly of humans as they tried to touch the sky. The intricate reliefs are in stark contrast to the large and severe carvings of the monument itself. The circular honorarium of words proclaims the glowing achievement of the Wrights. The giant rising sun is chiseled into the wing of the monument, which points toward the take off area far down the hill. Many people admire the doors and may wonder what the designs mean. Almost all who first arrived on the top of the hill have wondered why the doors are often closed and locked. The doors have been sealed off until recently to all entry since the 1960s. They seem to be closed to keep people out.

They may have been closed to keep something in.

The stories that were told about why the interior was closed off to tourists for so long usually include the tale that one of the visitors, when going up the narrow spiral staircase inside the monument, became stuck and panicked. Claustrophobia closed the granite walls in upon the person, and the dark stairwell seemed to seize the person in a grip of fear that they would never get out. The story is close to the truth.

But not quite.

The legend of the monument, untold even to this day, is that the person felt a real grip upon her shoulder. She thought it was the person behind her, as everyone that went up the hidden staircase to the viewpoint at the top struggled with the steep, difficult climb. She looked behind her. Instead of seeing a person on the step below, there was no person there. The visitor behind her had stopped to rest and had not even made the turn to be visible yet. No person stood behind her.

No full person.

Only a bony hand reached out to clutch at her shoulder. It gripped her, pinning her as it pushed down with an otherworldly strength. She found that she could not lift herself from the step to escape. Too terrified to go down past where the spectral arm reached out of the granite wall itself, and unable to go forward, she did the only thing she could.

She screamed.

It was an unnatural scream of sheer terror that cut through the stairs and stone all the way out the monument. People heard her outside. The line of people inside could barely move. It would take time before a ranger could get to her and calm the truly terrified woman.

Once outside, having told her tale, the visitor calmed slightly, though she desperately wanted to get off the hill and never come back. Since no one else saw the strange event, no one believed her. Everyone else assumed she either created the story or imagined it, and in her state of claustrophobia, her heightened panic had simply formed the image in her head. There was no way a disembodied arm reached out from the stone to pin down someone walking up the stairway.

Still, the Park Service had already been thinking of closing the door to the monument. It took work and people to guide tourists up and down the steep spiral staircase, which was certainly not designed for modern tourists in large numbers. Safety had become a more primary focus, and the new museum at the entrance was a more important draw than keeping the monument open.

The entrance also flooded when it rained, and had to be kept closed until the water could be cleaned out. The drain was installed poorly, and water did its share of damage to the insides. One of the busts of Wilbur and Orville, sitting in alcoves on the bottom floor, always was moving when it rained. No one could figure how the heavy cast copper busts were able to slip in their little display nooks. But it was noted, and plans for an additional display of the Wrights and their plane within the pylon were quickly shelved. When one of the busts was found on the floor, face first in inches of water, the decision was sealed. The monument would be closed.

Has the strange disembodied bony hand, floating through solid granite, been seen since, or even before? The few historians, reporters, and the Park Rangers that were able to go inside during the closure certainly haven't mentioned it. Ghosts and ghost stories are usually frowned upon by organizations that deal with "real" history. They leave the legends to others.

But there is one story that is never told about the monument. It happened before the big pylon was even built. From October of 1931 through November of 1932, the Army Corps of Engineers did the difficult work of building the monument. The granite blocks were cut at a quarry far inland from the Outer Banks at Mount Airy, NC, and brought to the coast. The final parts of the trip included carrying the multi-ton granite on barges through the sound to a canal to the south of the monument, where they were then lifted to a small train on a narrow railway, to be brought to the base of the hill and then lifted up and into place by a great crane.

The men that worked these jobs were strong, hardened, and diligent in their task. But accidents could and did happen. The Outer Banks was well known for its fickle and destructive storms that blew up from any direction, with little warning but a cold wind and a dark cloud, before dumping torrents of rain on unsuspecting people working outdoors. Such an event happened during the construction. On one of the barges, in an attempt to lift one of the giant granite blocks at the beginning of a particularly fast moving and dark storm, the straps holding the 4000 pound stone slipped as the barge wallowed in the shallow, muddy water. As careful as they were, there was no avoiding the giant block as it tumbled and fell first to the deck of the barge, then over the side into the murky brackish water. Sadly, one of the workers had been on the wrong side of the granite block. It was just unfortunate happenstance that the block fell the way it did. The poor man was crushed and killed instantly, before the block even hit the water.

The other workers were aghast as they tried to see if the man would come back up. But they knew, there was no saving him. He was surely dead by the falling stone. If not, there was no helping him from being pinned under the granite now embedded in the soft loamy mud of the sound.

When the water finally calmed from the upstart storm, and the waves subsided, they could look down into the brown water. In the shallows they could easily make out the giant piece of granite. On one side, in a vague outline, all they could see of their fellow laborer was his forearm and hand, reaching up from the depths where his dead body lay pinned in a watery grave.

To this day, few will discuss the spooky hand that reached out from the beyond. And then in hushed tones. They say his spirit stayed when his body left, and rode on another stone, used in replacement to the one that crushed him. Just like in his final moments, only his hand is visible. It would appear during or after a rain, which may have explained the immense flooding in the obelisk, or why the monument was always locked up during a storm.

The monument has been reopened now, at least at the bottom. There is no access to the top. It could be that the spirit of the man is finally at rest, after being locked away for so long, and the ghostly hand finally moved on. But the monument is only opened on sunny days, and it still floods during the rain.

Shadows Of Nags Head Woods

Nags Head

Nags Head Woods has been an overgrown pasture of mystery for over one hundred years now. The long stretch of undisturbed pine and hardwood interspersed with shallow freshwater pools is a contradictory wilderness on an Outer Banks that is well known for its open beaches and wide horizons. Abundant nature, the plentiful flora and fauna that are the mark of a truly wild space, are at a minimum on much of the developed coast. Nags Head Woods is a place where the song of the forest, wild with brambles and berries, can still be heard to be sung.

It would be unfair to say that it has always been this way, though. Nags Head Woods once was the center of life on the island, even at a much smaller capacity. This was the original setting for homes of the Bankers.

Most know the stories of the Banker people, who first arrived on the Outer Banks from shipwrecks just offshore. With nothing left except what they could possibly salvage from the water's edge, and no hope of rescue, they had the choice of sitting on the beach until they died or getting up and doing something about it. The will to live is strong, as is the fear of death, especially after escaping its cold grip from a shipwreck on a most unforgiving coast. It was no wonder these people settled as far away from the beach as possible.

Building a community on the west side of the Outer Banks actually made a lot of sense. It was far away from the open, rolling beaches with its unpredictable surf. Storms and hurricanes could come up in a day with no warning, snatching houses and people without a thought to be lost to the ocean. There were no dunes to protect them; these would come at least a hundred years later. Living in the protected woods slowed the cold winds and gave protection to the Bankers. Supplies may be scarce, but nature could provide, for a day or a week, with wood to burn or build, and fish, flora, and fowl to eat. It may not have been a secure life, but they lived as far from the precipice as they could.

Old Nags Head was the community of Nags Head Woods as well as the vacation cottages that were built south of Jockey's Ridge. The community grew and flourished. A house of God was turned into a church, hotels that had hundreds of rooms were built, with dance halls and bowling alleys. Long piers reached out from the shallows into the deeper parts of the sound to make it easy for larger boats to access the coastal lands. Even a road stretched from Jockey's Ridge all the way up the west of the island toward Kitty Hawk and the community that had formed there. The Bankers and their guests had found a way to take hold of the land and make a life there.

But where there was life, death was sure to follow. In so many ways.

By the 1850s, visitors had found a way to build on the beach, to enjoy the sunny beach life, at least in the summer, with little to fear from the fierce storms of the other seasons. It would take generations, but the communities and the people of Old Nags Head would slowly move away or die off. Then the homes, now empty, also began to die. They fell to disrepair, vandalism, sometimes fire, with only the foundations remaining to mark where they once stood. Soon, about the only things left to memorialize the history of Old Nags Head were the numerous small cemeteries that dotted the old sand and clay road which ran from Nags Head to Kill Devil Hills.

Nags Head Woods grew over the old town. With it, its legend grew, too. It was mysterious, old, hidden. The place was inaccessible and distant. Soon, the stories began. It was a gathering place for those who wanted to be unseen, with clandestine meetings for nefarious purposes. It later took on whatever popular urban legend would take hold at the time. Devil worship, witchcraft, and the spooky tale of the goat man all permeated the woods at some time.

Underneath all the legends, the urban myths that changed with the wind, there were more stories, told only in whisper so as not to anger the spirits that still resided in the old woods. Ghost lights flickered in the trees at night where homes once stood. While some waved them off as simple foxfire or will o' the wisp, old timers knew the lights were the remnants of past times. The spirits and memories of people who called the land home in the past still remained in the present.

Other stories were even less benign.

One tale speaks of an old cemetery, no longer a yard for graves as the church had long turned to dust and splinters. The only thing left were the graves. Ten graves sat in lines of three or four in a small nook off the old road, carved into the mix of the hard packed silt and gritty sand that blew over from the beach long ago. The soil is an ugly, clingy mix that is a sticky mud at the first sign of rain, but turns to a coating of dust when dry.

As nature found her home again in the land, a spindly wild maple tree found purchase in the middle of the cemetery. It grew directly up from one grave, giving shade and almost uprooting the old marker, now worn smooth with anonymity. The tree's roots grew down and into the shallow grave, to feed off the nutrients of the bodies.

But that's not all.

If someone goes to the cemetery, walks up to the tree, and starts to gently scratch it, give the tree a soft tickle, that feeling will go down the roots of the tree, into the grave, and into the body below.

And the corpse will start to laugh.

And the tree will start to shake.

This is usually a good time to leave.

Sadly, one time, a teenager didn't make the good choice. After hearing of the legend, on a dare, he went out to the tree. He was to go tickle the tree and see if it would tremble. To prove he had been there, he must carve his name in the tree. He had to leave a mark of some sort. So he went to try his luck.

He began to tickle the tree, and soon enough, it began to shake and tremble, as if it was shaking with laughter. Sure it was just the wind, or perhaps he had hooked a branch on his clothes, he dismissed the strange feeling and kept at it. Only when he heard the laughing did he realize that there was more to the legend, and that the story was true.

By now, the corpse was laughing through the earth. It could be heard plainly. Maybe the boy thought someone was playing a prank, or perhaps he just wanted to see what would happen next, but he didn't leave when he should have. Because once the corpse starts laughing, the rest of the cemetery wants to know what is so funny. And they all come up to see.

The boy was never seen again. The grave and the cemetery are all but gone now, taken by the forest of which it was once carved. The stone markers are still there, hidden in the grass and weeds. There are still ten of them, in three uneven rows.

But now there are eleven graves.

The Uncovered Grave

Buxton

Driving into Buxton on a windy evening, you will see her. A figure in gray, a woman, thin, older, in a long dress and jacket. She walks the side of the road with determination. Only she does not so much walk, as float. Seen from afar, she moves with a purpose, her body tense, her chin forward. No one knows what she looks like up close. If anyone gets too near, the figure disappears into the wind.

The fortunate few who have glanced this ethereal spirit are witness to the ghostly apparition of Nora Alice Farrow, who walks the roadside of Buxton on evenings when the wind blows hard and the storms churn the ocean. Her story begins not on land, but at sea.

The Graveyard of the Atlantic is a name befitting the churning currents just offshore Hatteras Island and the lonely Outer Banks. Wind and waves relentlessly pound against the hulls of ships. Shallow sandbars reach up to pin any vessel hard aground. The area has become well known as a home to countless shipwrecks. The watery graves of people lost from those ships are more numerous by multiples unable to figure. From 1585 with Sir Richard Grenville's first expedition from England, when his ship, *The Tiger*, right up to present day, ships have become stranded, cracked open, or capsized and sunk along the coast. When the storms couldn't capture a vessel, war brought its own danger. Tempests and torpedoes both sent ships to a sad end at the bottom of the Graveyard of the Atlantic.

For the longest time when shipwrecks occurred the bodies appeared ashore to be found by surprised and dismayed locals. There was no way to determine who these poor souls were, as the souls had already left the bodies long before. Most dead bodies were dragged to the dry part of the beach and buried in a shallow hole in the sand. For hundreds of years afterwards, especially after storms, where the low natural dunes of Cape Hatteras were cut and eroded in the harsh spring weather, people would find bones of old shipwreck victims and their hasty burials along the beach.

For a period of time, there was at least one person who fought against this action. Nora Alice Farrow was one of many long time residents of Cape Hatteras who were born to the children and grandchildren of other shipwreck survivors or pirates or whoever came ashore long before them. Nora

Alice was as strong willed and steadfast as a Banker woman had to be. Everyone earned their keep on the island if they could. She did her part by providing a clean home and well tended garden for her husband and her family. She also made sure that no one else went without if there was enough to share. She was forceful when needed, but kind at all times.

Nora Alice would often find herself walking the beaches, collecting whatever might wash up ashore. The locals were known to use whatever the sea was willing to part. Wood from ships was used to build their houses, pennants and sacks were blankets and clothes, and nothing was put to waste. She often collected driftwood on sunny days as it made an excellent fire when dry.

One day she came across a poor soul who had been once lost to the ocean, but now tossed ashore. Nora Alice, like most of the islanders, had seen their share of injury and death. While the body may be gruesome, she knew it once was a person with life and love. There was a story to the person more than their death, she knew. When some local boys came over to see the body, she ordered them to take the corpse across the dunes to dry land to bury it. One went back to Nora Alice's home to get an old blanket and some shovels, then the two, under Nora Alice's watchful eye, did their best to give a proper burial to the departed.

The people of Hatteras were, if not accustomed, at least understanding that death could be near at hand for anyone. A passing could come quickly, from illness or from an accident, and they had all experienced both at some time. A wake and a quick funeral were the best that they could often do, as the bodies did not last long in the salt and sun. They did what they could as a community to honor the dead, and move on. Nora Alice thought that it was no less a task to perform for the people she didn't know who lost their lives offshore.

Soon, she would be seen walking the beaches in the cold spring weather, when the winds blew hard from the north and the sea foam rolled across the sand. Tall and thin, wearing a long gray dress and warm cloak, she walked with her face up into the bitter wind, searching the coast after a shipwreck to make sure no bodies were untended if they washed ashore. If she found someone, she would arrange to have them carried across the dunes and buried in the shade of trees and yaupon bushes that dotted the more protected land. The edge of Trent Woods, thick with trees and mysterious with ghosts of its own, soon became a final resting place for the lost. No grave markers were made, as no names were known. The best the islanders could do was a pile of shells or a whelk planted as a headstone, mostly to mark where a body was so it wouldn't be dug up in the future.

When she could, Nora Alice would say a few words over the grave. She would tell the person they were safe from the storm and that even if she didn't know their name, that they would be remembered. Over the years Nora Alice figured she had helped plant the spirit of over a hundred souls.

When she got older, she couldn't go out as often, but still insisted that the bodies be recovered and buried properly. "We would want the same for our families," she insisted. When she could no longer go out, she would remind the younger people to be on the lookout, and to carry on her wishes.

Nora Alice Farrow lived to a ripe old age of 77, passing away in 1875. Many locals took note that the U.S. Lifesaving Service had only recently been created, and several stations now covered the islands of the Outer Banks. Her job was now done, and now done by others. Brave men would train and practice to be ready to go out on a moment's notice to save the lives before they were lost. Nora Alice wouldn't have to patrol the beaches any more.

Nora Alice was buried in one of the many small family cemeteries that fit into small open spots along the towns of Buxton and Frisco. In accordance to her wishes, due to her walking the beach often, she asked that the top foot of her grave be covered with sand, above the chunky loam that made up the soil beyond the shore. No one really knew why, but they honored her request.

It would be about ninety years before anyone would take notice of her grave again. In 1962, Highway 12 from Nags Head to Hatteras would be built. The paved road opened up the once isolated community, and also bisected the town, with the east shore side and the protected sound side split. Nora Alice's grave and the whole cemetery were now just exposed enough to let the cold north winds blow in.

Soon, people began to spot a woman walking on the side of the road near the entrance to the villages of Hatteras. She was an old woman in a long gray dress. She never crossed the road. She always had the look of someone who was frustrated, and searching for something or someone. The figure only appeared at dusk and into the dark, never during the day. She was seen fitfully. The old lady never followed a schedule.

It took a long time for some to notice that she appeared more often in spring and winter than other times. She was especially visible and animated after a storm or when the wind blew hard. Certainly she was a ghost, the locals realized. She disappeared without a word. No one could find any living old woman walking around at night. After long searches, someone finally realized that it was Nora Alice Farrow. Locals discovered that her grave, old and weathered, had smoothed itself out but still had a deep divot where the sand had been placed. When the wind blew and storms raged during the rough spring weather, the sand from her grave would be spun out of its home to scatter to the winds. In the summer, the calm breezes and warm west winds helped pile the sand up and keep her grave still. It followed the same pattern as the beaches. The sand would fill up in the summer and rest there, until the winter cold and spring storms pulled the sand away.

Nora Alice would then walk only when her grave was uncovered.

Locals finally found the story of her life. They figured that her ghost is not really at unrest. She is only out to remind the living to continue her quest. She wants to make sure her grave, as with all the ones over which she had stood in life, were still covered, and the dead respected. When the wind blows, she walks, until someone comes to recover her final resting place.

Mad Mabe And The Viking Fisherman
Nags Head

Stories about witches living along the Outer Banks are about as common as the sand in our houses. Everybody has a lot of them. Witches and magic spells and curses and herbal medicine are part and parcel of the collection of legends that make up the history of the coast. From Cora the witch down in Hatteras or the Sea Hag of Portsmouth Island there are tales and stories of little old ladies living alone on the soundside shores, whispering up a charm or cackling out a curse on someone who did them wrong. Some might have truly been witches, while others might have just been nice little old ladies with clean houses and worn brooms to show for it, and they appreciated the attention they got for their antics.

One such witch, though she never would admit it, lived fairly recently in a house on the Roanoke Sound. Even the Wright Brothers knew of her, learning about the old woman in the woods on their first trips to the Outer Banks. Mad Mabe was already a legend when the brothers walked the woods and explored the barrier island while not working on their kites and gliders.

She was called Miss Mabe to her face, and whenever she may have been in earshot of the fishermen and families that lived on the sound. Far from shore, or behind a closed door, her nickname "Mad Mabe" might have been uttered, but even then with a tall glass of concern and possible furtive glances, just to make sure it wouldn't get back to the old woman. It was definitely not said around the children. Little pitchers had big ears, and wide mouths to pour out anything that they heard.

Miss Mabe loved little children. They loved her, too. She would often read their palms or tell fortunes for a penny. The kids would scrounge for change around stores or along the beaches to give her. She would happily tell them of a coming reward, candy or treats, or some form of success at school, but always something good. Occasionally giving them sweets herself made sure that at least some of her prophecies would come true.

The neighbors loved Miss Mabe, as well, when she was Miss Mabe. A sweet old lady who was gracious when receiving help was a pleasant neighbor. Fishermen who went out onto the sound for their catch would often come by her dock to leave a present for the woman who was not able to go out herself. Some crabs in a bucket, a mess of shrimp, or a fish or two were all that were needed to placate the woman.

But they all hated Mad Mabe.

When she became Mad Mabe, bad things happened. If a fisherman didn't have much luck, or came in late, or somehow just forgot to leave a gift on Mabe's dock, she would notice the slight immediately. Then she would turn sour and cross. Neighbors would see her circling her home, muttering or cursing. Sometimes she would light an old rag on fire and wave it around, just in case no one noticed her bad temper. And within a day, the winds would change.

The wind would shift, no longer from the south or west, but from the northeast. It would be colder, a biting wind, and often the sound would empty out into shallow channels. The boats would no longer be able to get out, and the fish would not be there.

Usually the fishermen would get together and reveal that one or more of them had forgotten to give a tribute to Miss Mabe, and she became Mad Mabe. While she may or may not have been a witch, it was dangerous to tempt fates, so a group would go visit her and ask for forgiveness, along with a gift, in hopes that the winds would change. While Miss Mabe denied causing the ill wind, she always said that she would see what she could do.

And with that, the winds lifted again.

Now, most people figured this was a prudent action to take care of a part of their community, as well as a bit of protection, just in case. Fishermen are by nature a superstitious lot. There is much that can go wrong, and everything that has to go right, when fishing for a living, so they take no chances. But there is more than just witches that worry them.

One fisherman that lived on the sound was Arne Holman. He was a Scandinavian who showed up with his boat and some lumber and simply settled in to the life of a Banker fisherman. He was different than the others, not only by his looks and mannerisms, but by his boat as well. The native watermen all depended upon the shad boat as their means of sailing. It was a wide and comfortable flat bottom boat that worked well in the sound waters. His boat was a long curved peapod of a sailboat, complete with the painted decorations of flowers and vines on the bow.

Arne talked differently, definitely looked different, and had a different boat. Even his name was so unique to the Bankers that he became Arnie Holliman to them. He had his strange quirks. There were little things he did that no other fisherman would do. He had his own versions of good luck charms and rituals. The locals would sometimes just tolerate his strangeness. But sometimes he did things that made them shiver.

There is a curious act of bad luck, a dangerous activity that most sailors won't do on board a boat. Sailors don't whistle while sailing. It's considered more than bad luck. It is as if the sailor is challenging the wind itself. Whistling means a sailor thinks they can make their own winds. If someone whistles on a boat, the wind will stop, and they will be stranded in the water.

But Arnie Holliman could whistle up a wind.

When the wind wouldn't blow, or it was too light, he could be seen on the bow of his sailboat, lips pursed as he sang out a haunting tune. Then, regular as a clock, a dark patch would form far off in the water behind him. It would race up to his boat, and the sails would snap and the rigging would sing tight, and he would be off. His little peapod could go in shallow water or deep, and with the help of a bit of wind, Arnie could get just about anywhere to get his catch. So when others came up with a meager take, Arnie always had something more.

The problem was, Arnie felt like he earned his catch, and he used his own magic to do so. He didn't like to share.

When he would come back with other fishermen, he would begrudgingly leave some donation, just to appease his neighbors. If he came back alone, he purposefully would skip Miss Mabe's dock. Then Miss Mabe could be seen, plotting, pacing, tramping around, mad at the slight. Usually others would go appease her with a treat. That wouldn't always work. So Miss Mabe became Mad Mabe, and the storms started brewing.

Now, when the wind stopped, the boats wouldn't go out. Except for Arnie's. He would be seen, poling his little peapod out to the channel, then he would whistle up a wind, and off he would go. No one knew how he did it. They all called him a crazy "Scandihoovian" under their breath and wondered what magic he used to find the fish once he got his sails filled. But just as they were afraid of the dark side of Mad Mabe, so too were they concerned with the strange magic of Arnie Holliman.

The winds would come back, as they always did, whether through the influence of Miss Mabe or that they finally shifted, no one could tell back then. Everything would go back to normal.

Until again Arnie Holliman skipped by Miss Mabe's dock.

And again.

Miss Mabe had had it. She stormed out, mad as a cat, hissing and cursing as she circled her house. She lit her rag of fire and called up the winds to blow from the cold northeast. This would ruin fishing and everything else for days. She waved her burning rag on a stick and shouted for the winds to come. And of course, they obeyed.

The rest of the villagers, fishermen and everyone else, planned some act of contrition that would appease her. But they knew only one gesture would really help. Arnie Holliman had to give up his catch and apologize. The townsfolk gathered a respectful crew of citizens to politely ask Arnie to pay a visit to Miss Mabe. When they got to his cabin, with its own strange decorations of painted flowers and vines in green and yellow, they found him gone. Trouble was in the air, mixed with the cold north winds that howled through the trees. For they saw that Arnie had gone out in his boat in the storm.

He had poled his way out of the muddy shallows that now extended far off from the long docks of all the soundside houses of Nags Head. He found the channel and stood, clutching his mast, lips almost in a smile as he called up his own wind. Far on the shore, the locals couldn't hear the tune, but they knew what was going to happen. A dark patch of water, with a solid wind above it, blew against the tempest and caught Arnie's boat, filling the sail and sending him racing away. He quickly disappeared into the far reaches of Roanoke Sound to fill his little boat full of crabs, shrimp, and fish.

This enraged Miss Mabe even more when she saw him come in with his boat filled with fish. He had to get out and drag it over the mud flats the last bit of distance to his dock, before tying it up and unloading his catch.

He only made it worse by doing it again the next day.

By the third day, everyone but Arnie had seen enough. Arnie enjoyed having fish to sell when others didn't, but no one else was happy at all. Especially Miss Mabe. When Arnie whistled up a wind this day, Mad Mabe appeared, her rag soaked in lamp oil flaming over her head, bits of it whipped off by the wind, as she screeched over the sounds of the gale. She was going to show old Arnie just what she could do, even though she was just a little old lady, and not a witch.

The skies grew dark, losing even the cold white overcast look. This was a swirling storm of wind and rain, sheets of it, flying across the open sound like curtains shutting on the world. Arnie stood on his boat, in the middle of it. No one could hear him, but they all wondered if he had a song to face off against this much of a storm. A black line of water came up from his back and raced toward the darkening front, splitting it just enough that his little boat wouldn't be capsized. Then, no one knew what happened after that. The boat and the whole sound were covered in a horrible storm.

It lasted all day, and into the evening. The sound filled, then flooded. People lost their docks as the wooden structures floated away. Boats snapped their lines. The craft were thrown into the woods by the flooding water or tipped over by churning waves. Several washed away down past the old causeway and into the marshes near Bodie Island Lighthouse, never to be found again.

The houses of Nags Head, never structurally sound to begin with, began to leak, then pour. Families ran out of buckets after a while. They couldn't even open the windows to throw out the water full in their pans. It would let more water in than out. Everyone wanted to do something, anything to stop the deluge, but it seemed impossible. Unless someone had an ark hidden in the forest, there was nothing they could do except wait.

The storm finally gave up its last. The sheets of rain fell to a mist, then a trickle, then the skies opened to a clear cold night with stars slowly twinkling on in the heavens. The locals noted, quietly, that with it being night, there was no rainbow, and no promise this wouldn't happen again.

One of the most respected fishermen of the village struggled out of his house. It was caked in mud and pine needles from the storm. He had to make a pilgrimage to Miss Mabe's house. He had nothing to give her. He was just going to plead with her to make it stop, for the sake of the families.

When he got there, he found her house was as much in shambles as all the rest. A big tree branch had fallen, cracking open the roof and letting the storm pour in on the old woman. She sat forlornly in her little cottage, shaken and ashamed, but still with a hint of pride.

The fisherman begged her to stop. The storm had caused so much destruction, even to her own home, that it wasn't worth the damage. He promised extra catch for her in the future. He even said he would convince the other watermen to do the same. Anything for her to lift her curse.

Miss Mabe was conscience-stricken. She hadn't meant to harm the families and children. She liked them, really. It was just that selfish Scandihoovian, Arnie, who scoffed at her skills with his own magic.

What would he do?

The fisherman felt bad about what he had to tell her. He didn't think that Miss Mabe actually meant to hurt anyone. She just was an old woman who had her pride wounded. Arnie Holliman was gone. No one had seen him since he vanished in the storm, he told her. It was unlikely he was still alive. He probably drowned in the storm.

Miss Mabe felt terrible about what she had done. She never meant to hurt him. Her pride had caused her to act up, even though she always claimed she didn't do any magic. She knew she had sent poor Arnie to a watery grave.

As good fortune would have it, Arnie was found, alive, but shaken, the next day. His boat had been tossed over and pushed into Nags Head Woods. Oddly, it had moved against the wind, to the north, while all the water had blown away from that same direction. He stoically confessed that perhaps he had whistled up a bit too much wind, and his luck and charm had pushed him too far. He was cut and injured from his strange shipwreck, but with help he was able to free his boat and get back to his home.

His house was as badly damaged as the others. The wind had whipped around it so hard that the paint had come off, and now it was only covered with green pine needles. His dock, like all the rest, was gone, floating away somewhere halfway to Oregon Inlet by now.

After a week of repairs to the homes on the sound, things were better, if not back to normal. Most of the boats would be repaired, and at least one long dock was rebuilt that they could share until their own piers could be fixed. The day finally came when the fishermen were back able to go out onto the water.

It was a perfect morning to be on the water. The sound was slick, with barely a lap of waves on the hulls as they sat tied to the dock. A soft wind, warm, blew from the west. West, when fishing was best, they would say. The families gathered at the shore to watch as the wide flat bottom boats all put up their sails and began to slowly cut through the oiled glass that was the Roanoke Sound that day. It was important to them to be there. The ceremony and beauty of it would be seen by any visitor, but the locals knew that they had to go out. This was their life, how they survived.

The boats had barely made any time in the light wind. At least it was a nice day. Then they all heard it. There was a mysterious song being sung on the wind. Sailor and family alike looked to see where it came from. In the midst of the flotilla came a tiny peapod boat, round and curved where the shad boats of the locals were wide and straight sided. Arnie Holliman stood on the bow and whistled a tune. Soon, a black patch appeared behind the boats. It split and spread, going out to all of them. The sails snapped and the rigging sang as the brackish water sprayed off the tightening lines. It would be a good day for fishing.

At the end of the day, the fishermen all came home with their craft heavy and full to the gunwales. In turn, each stopped at Miss Mabe's house with a gift of one of their best catch. One by one they sailed in to present it. As the sun set, turning the sky a burning orange at the horizon while the stars began to twinkle in a cool purple twilight, one more boat passed. The curved vessel set a distinctive and unique shadow of its profile as it slowed at her dock. Two more fish, large, shiny, found their way upon the end of her pier. Then the boat sped off into the darkness.

In the cool of the evening, as the land breezes took over, the people of the village swore they heard a bit of music whistling through the night air.

Nuova Ottavia

Corolla

It was May, and I had bought my first car, a new Jeep CJ-7. I was nearing my twentieth birthday. I decided to forgo the usual tumult of four wheeling on the sand roads of Nags Head Woods or driving around Run Hill behind the Wright Brothers Monument and truly do some exploring. I drove up to Corolla with my dog, a brown and white boxer named Prospero. I wondered what he thought about being named after a shipwreck victim while being a beach dog, but he probably didn't care as long as he got ear scratches and frisbees to chase.

This was back before Corolla was developed. It was all sand and twisty dunes, with a few people up there trying to sell property that didn't even have much of a road yet. I just wanted to see the lighthouse and find some of the old homes that used to be up there. Armed with my camera, my tent, a few books and maps, and more food than I could possibly eat in a day, we headed up the coast.

I camped out on an open hill near the beach. The old Currituck Lighthouse stood dead and unlit behind my shoulder as I pitched my tent on an open topped bald dune. The wind blew fiercely, but I knew that was a good thing. It would keep the mosquitoes away. No sea grass around my site would hopefully mean none of the wild Corolla Banker ponies to show up, either. This was their land, and I was the interloper. I had no desire to trespass on their home more than I already had.

I took Prospero out the the beach to let him run after the long trip. He seemed eager to get out and roll in the fresh salty sand, finding all the strange scents of the beach as he bounded up in the air. I understood that feeling. It's the same way I feel when the beach first warms up and it is still empty, before summer hits and the circus comes to town.

We ran down the beach, past the old dilapidated lifesaving station that was built at the turn of the century. At one time it had been the working home for a number of brave and tough men who would go out and save the lives of shipwrecked sailors. Now it sat empty. The winds of the years had peeled much of the paint off the siding, and sand piled up at the ocean side door. I was surprised it still stood.

Along the dunes, I could see the occasional pony, standing watch like a pirate on a hill, on the lookout for the colonial navy to come down from Virginia to get them. I worried that Prospero, feeling his freedom, would take off after one of the horses, flying like a canary to the sun, never to be seen again. But a strange thing happened to him. As he was tearing down the hard packed beach, just above the slow whoosh of the ocean wash upon the shore, suddenly, he stopped.

I caught up to him quickly to attach his leash in case he bolted, but I didn't need to worry. At least, I didn't need to worry about him running off. He sat still, his fur bristling, a low growl coming from his throat that would end with the beginning of a whimper. Then he would repeat the sounds. He looked both terrified and vicious. I couldn't figure out what made him so scared.

I thought at first it was one of the horses, but they had all left the hills. We were alone, as far as the eye could see. A dark blue ocean was creased where rolling waves hit a sandbar far offshore, only to reform into a blue-green foam until it rolled onto the beach, in more of a whisper than a crash. Not even a cloud dotted the soft pastel blue sky that folded neatly into the horizon far, far away. Prospero stared out into an empty sea, taut as a sailing rope.

I carefully hooked up his leash, and with a soft tug, said, "C'mon, boy, let's go."

With a huff, he gave in and turned with me, his shoulder tight against my knee, his head on a constant swivel looking back at a flat and empty sea.

We got back to the camp, and while Prospero ate his dog food gravely, with the occasional sniff into the wind, I read some of my books to see what I could find. I knew about the old towns that used to be here. Corolla was originally Jones Hill, and there was also the tiny town of Seagull. That little village farther north had been swallowed whole by the march of the sand dunes. What was left was buried under mounds of sand and scrub brush. There even was an ancient maritime forest that grew out of the beach. It was nothing but bare tree stumps now, but it marked what once was the west side of the Outer Banks.

Farther north, another lifesaving station stood. The old Wash Woods station was probably in the same condition as this one, and I had no need to drive up farther to see it. There were legends that it was haunted. A member of the old Coast Guard still haunted the place, along with his favorite black horse. But I knew that was just hokum. One of my friends had told me it was just legend to scare people out of going in and vandalizing the place.

As the sun began to sink over the sound, the sky above turned deep orange, while the horizon over the ocean began to change to a murky purple. Far to the west, the red brick lighthouse turned to silhouette, and cast an immense shadow far across the island. It looked like it was reaching out, for me, for the beach, the ocean. The feeling was quite unnerving.

I had gone out to gather some driftwood for a fire. Prospero and I had stumbled upon a large open area that had several mounds in the wild grass covered land. It looked a little like a cemetery, but without any headstones. I knew that the victims of shipwrecks were often buried on the shore where they were found. I thought it was rather sad for them. They lose their lives in a terrible catastrophe, only to have their remains buried without even a name to remember them. And no family would ever mourn over their grave. Over time, they would be lost forever.

But then, on the other hand, it was a rather nice piece of land to have if you had to do the Big Sleep.

Night fell quickly, and it got cold just as fast. I built a small fire out of the driftwood in a pit in the sand. By the firelight, I glanced over the old shipwreck maps to see if anything was left on the beach up here. The only ones I found were the *Metropolis*, an ancient sailing vessel that was pretty famous, and one I hadn't heard of, the *Nuova Ottavia*.

It was a big ship, which surprised me even more that I hadn't heard of it. An Italian barque, a big three masted ship, had run aground here in the 1870s when they mistook the new Currituck Lighthouse for the Cape Henry Light and turned for Caffey's Inlet, only to be grounded on a sandbar about four hundred yards offshore. I was surprised this wasn't more famous. I couldn't find any information on what happened to the ship. If it cracked up in the sea, it might still be out there somewhere. The Atlantic was the final home to hundreds, maybe thousands, of sunken ships and their crews.

I watched the fire slowly die out as darkness came in fully to engulf the beach. The evening turned into a cloudy, moonless night, with stars only coming out sporadically, fighting the overcast haze and losing. Down on the beach, I could see the orange and yellow reflection of my fire in the old, broken panes in the windows of the abandoned lifesaving station. No one had told me any stories about that place. I had no idea if it was haunted or not, but the reflection of the flames in salt covered windows created a vaguely otherworldly motion that looked as if the crew were back again, moving around inside as if they were responding to a call of distress. But there were no ships on the ocean that night, and if the ghosts were moving, they never made it past the doors to the beach.

I went to the beach to get a bucket of salt water for the fire. It might have been early in the evening, but I had nothing else to do but read, so I decided to put the fire out and climb into my sleeping bag. Walking back, I swore I heard noises, not coming from inside the old station, but farther off. Again, Prospero tensed and growled into the nothingness around us.

Back at the camp, I doused and stirred the embers of my fire before climbing into the tent. At first I thought it would be better to leave the big lamp on inside the tent, just to chase the monsters away from outside. Then I realized I was lighting myself up as a beacon, and I wouldn't see anything coming from the darkness. I had to admit it, I was a little spooked. I turned off the big lamp and lit my flashlight. Its orange glow was slightly more comforting. My collection of maps and ghost tales looked particularly disagreeable at this moment, so I instead curled up with Prospero at my feet and listened to the soft crash of the ocean, hoping to hear nothing behind it.

By ten o'clock, both man and beast were tired, so I switched the light off and went to sleep. The waves had lulled my senses. The wind whistled tunelessly across the shore. It was a hypnotic white noise that blurred the outside world from my brain. I fell into a dark and dreamless sleep.

I had slept for not quite two hours when my head began to play tricks on me. I was sure I heard a tapping upon my door, which was quite impossible on the canvas tent. I couldn't tell if my eyes were open or not. Everything was dark. There were no lights to make the land glow. In my foggy mind, I heard voices from far off.

I finally awoke enough to figure out the tapping sound. Prospero was up, walking back and forth from the zipper door to the window and back. His ears were pinned and he was on guard, a concerned whimper mixed with a growl. Someone, several people, were outside on the beach. Not near, but not too far, either. I could hear their muffled shouting as it carried over the sand.

With the creeping fear I had earlier, I didn't take my flashlight, but did go outside the tent to see what was happening. My curiosity outweighed my unease. I held Prospero tight until I got his leash on, then wrapped it around my wrist tightly before giving him an urgent and quiet command to stay.

At first I saw very little. I only heard the sounds.

There was yelling, a series of confused commands. The words were lost in the salt air, but the sound was defined. Orders, stressed imperatives carried to us from the dark. Over the sound of the shouts came splashes and scrapes of something being dragged across the wet sand. In front of us, the lifesaving station sat dead, dull, a bare block in an inky black night. No one was near there.

Prospero saw the lights first. A red and green glow came from far out to sea, about three or four hundred yards. Then another, onshore, brighter, a red beacon coming from a lamp. It bobbed like it floated above the waves but also moved by them. I couldn't see anything holding the strange ethereal light. It lurched over the waves, and bounced as if upon an invisible mast of a boat. The light moved quickly out to the others that floated over the sandbar. It took minutes for the orbs to finally meet up.

The bobbing red light circled the other lamps. Then, with a suddenness that surprised me and made poor Prospero jump with a yelp, the red light seemed to topple into the ocean and be extinguished. More unintelligible shouting happened, even more desperate, almost a lament or wail.

I wanted to run to the sounds. I was unsure of what had happened, and I felt like I needed to help in some way. I took a furtive step forward. Prospero pulled back. His body settled into the sand, ready to anchor itself to keep me from moving. Prospero had always been a rather brave dog, never foolhardy, but definitely protective of me. The feeling he gave out, a decidedly concerned whine, made me stop. "C'mon, Pros," I cooed to him with a tug of his leash, "they may need help."

But the dog wouldn't budge. He knew something I didn't. There was no helping the people that were out there now. I knelt to comfort him, my eyes still on the sounds from far off of people crying in a strange panic.

Suddenly, Prospero fell to the sand, his paws over his head. Foolishly, I looked up instead of following his warning. I was rewarded by the sound of a loud high pitched cough. The explosion came from the beach, though I saw no light. The sound was an unnerving booming crack, like someone threw explosives in a metal can.

Prospero was up now, and so was I. We both ran to the only protection we had, my brand new Jeep. As we huddled behind the front wheel, I realized my keys sat inside my tent, which at twenty feet away seemed like an open mile. I had no idea if someone was shooting at us or throwing dynamite or if it was an invasion. I was barefoot and shirtless in a dark land that was a day's walk to any other human contact, let alone help. I thought of running for my keys, just to get in the Jeep and driving away as fast as I could, when another booming cough came across the beach.

Two more explosions would crease the winds, loud, short, desperate.

That was enough for me. I ran for the tent, whipped open the unzipped door and fumbled for my keys in the dark. I grabbed them, my shirt, and my flashlight and left. Any moment I knew that a shot from the booming gun would come ripping through my tent or tearing across my new Jeep. I got out and ran to the truck where Prospero sat in the passenger seat. If he could have fastened his seat belt himself, I truly think he would.

I started the engine; the rough roar of the Jeep cranking up seemed to be inordinately loud. It must have been heard as far as Virginia. I winced at the sound, but concentrated on purposefully not turning on the lights. I knew if I turned around completely, there was a soft sand road leading to the lighthouse and escape. I just had to be careful not to get stuck. Gunning the engine, I felt the wheels spin some in the soft ground, then finally bite. It was a terrifying moment of heart stopping paralysis where I feared I made enough noise to be noticed, but then would be stuck in the soft sand and unable to escape.

But the Jeep's tires took hold, and I controlled my panic enough to get the vehicle going. I circled the low hill, abandoning my tent and everything in it. A less dark path of sand appeared to my adjusted eyes, cutting through the trees that lined each side. I drove severely, not looking back. I concentrated solely on putting distance between us and the noises.

The noises.

It took me until I got to the main road to realize I heard nothing once the fourth blast occurred. I didn't know if I had scared them away. They certainly scared me. In my haste, I realized I had abandoned my camera and my wallet in the tent. My dander got up a little, along with my bravery. I didn't like being scared off. I wasn't too proud of myself, even if I would never tell this story to any of my friends, that I ran when I heard strange noises in the dark. I looked at Prospero, glowing in the light of the dash, and turned my amber lights on, just enough to see in front of me. I pulled into a copse of trees, faced the road, and turned my Jeep off. I decided to wait and see who came off the beach, especially if they left with any of my stuff. I wasn't going to be able to sleep, anyway.

I sat there, in the netherworld between sleep and awake, until morning.

At sunrise I awoke from an uncomfortable and fitful sleep of nightmares with pirates chasing me from out of the darkness. The Jeep had been a very uncomfortable bed. No one had passed to awaken me from my slumbers in the night, nor had anyone disturbed my campsite.

Curious, I wandered out to the beach to see what had caused the commotion. The tide line had come up, but the fair calm weather had done nothing to the beach. It was as smooth and unmolested as the day before. I found the marks of where Prospero and I had played, and where I had wandered down to get water for the fire, but nothing else. No tire tracks, no footprints, nothing. I felt my skin start to crawl up my back. I wondered if I had been the unwitting witness to a supernatural event.

I decided that I would pack up and leave as soon as possible. I needed to be in civilization again, as well as a real bed. As I packed the tent, I discovered my book open to a chapter on shipwrecks, specifically the *Nuova Ottavia*. I had left the book closed when the night came in, I know. I paused to read the brief report.

The *Nuova Ottavia* was an Italian barque, a big three masted ship, that had run aground on March 1, 1875. The captain had been sailing by dead reckoning, and had mistaken the newly constructed Currituck Beaches Lighthouse for Cape Henry, and had turned port to make for Caffey's Inlet.

The ship grounded hard upon the shoals offshore in fair weather in the late evening.

The Jones Hill Lifesaving Station had only been operating one season, and had already closed down, as the threat of rough winter seas had now ended. Only a skeleton crew remained, and they had been ill-prepared to do a rescue due to little training and experience. Five men took off in a life boat to aid the ship, at around 7:30 pm. They hauled a line to be used to help transfer the crew to shore. The little lifeboat circled the *Nuova Ottavia*, but when they crossed again in front of the bow, the life boat was pulled by the taut rope, and waves rushing around the Italian ship flooded it, capsizing the boat and spilling out the rescuers, including a volunteer from the lighthouse that offered to man an oar. In their haste, none had put on the cork life jackets that would have helped them survive the March sea waves. They would be found within hours or a day, all sadly drowned in the salt waters of the Atlantic.

With all the men from the lifesaving station now lost, the few locals who had come to the shore now became desperate. Unskilled in any way on how to rescue the men onboard the ship, they found and fired the small breeches buoy gun, a tiny cannon that shot a line to a ship so that the victims could then slide to shore on an attached seat. Unsure how to operate it, they fired blindly, four times, until the cannon was filled with sand and inoperable.

The *Nuova Ottavia* broke up the following day, and the remaining crew were able to make it ashore on the wreckage. Sadly, they communicated that five of the crew had died during the stranding, but all survivors of the initial wreck were able to come ashore. This meant that the attempt to rescue the men aboard the *Ottavia* would have saved no lives, as all the ship's crew alive on the ship had made it safely to the beach. The sailors who died aboard ship were buried in a makeshift cemetery just north of the station.

I finally realized what it was we had seen and heard. It was a haunted display from the past. The ship, stranded offshore, and the red light of the little lifesaving boat that capsized, all the yelling, screaming, and terror. And finally, in desperation, the firing of the little mortar, the buoy line, all done that night, again, as it happened all those years ago.

It was a somber ride back home. I thought about the choices the men had to face. They were all willing to go out to save others, as that was their job and duty, but they also made mistakes. These weren't the mistakes one can brush off to inexperience or poor youthful judgement. It was a difficult realization for me. I was growing up, ending my teenage years. I had made mistakes, too, and had to learn some things the hard way, with real repercussions. At least I got to learn from them, and to keep growing up. Becoming an adult was going to be a hard task. It was a terrifying lesson that had been thrown at me the night before.

I checked my speed, slowed down, and tightened my seat belt. Then I drove home into a bright and clear morning.

Ghosts And Spirits
Buffalo City

Buffalo City is now just an old ghost town, more name than place anymore, that sits deep in the forests of mainland Dare County. Its only residents are the deer and bear that wander the woods, black cottonmouth water moccasins that glide through the canals, and prodigious mosquitoes, thirsty for blood in the heat of summer. It used to be a flourishing company town, built by rich logging businesses to take down trees and pay a pittance in pluck, or company money. When the trees came down and the money dried up, the company left town.

Then all that was left were the ghosts and the spirits.

The spirits were liquor. When the jobs disappeared, the locals had to find a way to make money. During Prohibition, a good way, though not easy, was to make illegal whiskey. Buffalo City Whiskey was very good.

The benefits of the location for making moonshine were many. It was out in the middle of nowhere, hidden from the prying eyes of Treasury Men, out to hunt the stills. The local water was clean and tannic, great for making liquor. And the rye they used made a smooth, clean whiskey, popular with the drinking public up north that knew it by name. It wasn't unusual to see a long black car cruise into Buffalo City to carry on an illicit deal with a backwoods moonshiner.

That was the spirits.

The ghosts were another matter entirely.

The first ghosts were the moonshiners themselves. When Buffalo City made a name for itself, it also made itself a target. The revenuers would show up to hunt the moonshiners. It was not a fair nor respectful fight. Getting caught had grave consequences, including prison or getting shot. For the still operators, it was worth the risk. They made whiskey to make money so they could survive, so their families could eat. But getting caught was likely a sentence worse than death. A long prison term and no one to take care of the family was a horrible outcome. So the moonshiners became ghosts.

When the revenue men showed up with weapons and axes and explosives, they hunted down the stills. They chopped and burned them, pouring the liquor out in massive amounts, until it soaked the ground and flooded the creeks and canals of the old lumber town. It was so much that the fish even got drunk and died in the water. But they couldn't catch the people. Those moonshiners were ghosts. Wraiths. Spooks. Nothing but clouds and smoke. The government men knew they were there. They could feel the eyes on them. But they were never seen. The ghosts always got away.

One of the things that the moonshiners did to keep their liquor hidden during shipment was to take it out by boat. Little motorboats were numerous on the sound, along with their sail powered sisters. Every fisherman and crabber had a small boat to go out and catch food to eat or sell. The moonshiners blended right in. Instead of hauling the liquor in vats on the boats, they simply sealed the bottles well, tied them all to a long line, and trailed them out behind the boats. A trip to Elizabeth City or Edenton may be a long day's affair, but it would be profitable. And if the revenuers showed up to stop them on the sound, a simple flick of a knife, and the illegal hooch went to the bottom of the shallow water. If they wanted to, they could recover the moonshine, but making more was just as easy. They were ghosts. They had an eternity.

Eternity is a mighty long time. Even Prohibition ended. World War II and prosperity drew people out of the last hidden places with well paying jobs. Buffalo City's ghosts did their best to help satisfy the needs when towns stayed dry, but soon, Buffalo City saw its last inhabitant. It truly became a ghost town.

And every good ghost town needs ghosts.

The history and legends of Buffalo City stayed well hidden for a time. Then it opened up again as an adventure spot for kayakers and canoeists, along with hikers, explorers, and hunters. When the stories came back, so did the ghosts. Late in the night, people have seen strange lights deep in the juniper forests. Will-o'-the-Wisp, swamp gas, a fool's lantern, all these mysterious lights have drawn many a person into the woods, hypnotized by the light. That is the usual explanation of the lights seen in the woods there. The cause of the lights are never found, as they disappear whenever a hiker gets close. People swear that the lights are from phantom stills, continually in operation even in the afterlife. The ghosts had an eternity, remember?

Others have had less benign interactions. While most visitors go to enjoy the glassy waters in kayaks, some are out for treasure. Finding an old broken jug or a pluck coin meant to be spent at the company store is a rare event. Some people tried to dredge for the more devilish prize of a string of Buffalo City liquor, cut from a boat on the way to be sold in speakeasies far to the north. When people have found them, they have returned to their vehicles to find all the air out of their tires, or their windows covered with dust and soil. The tires aren't cut, only deflated. And the cars aren't dirty, just the windows. The ghosts don't like what they did, but they don't want anyone sticking around longer than wanted. They just don't want them to come back.

And leave the liquor.

The Postmaster's Amenity

Manteo

There are scary ghosts that appear in darkened halls as mysterious specters to glide across the old wooden floors of haunted houses, then disappear as they pass through a solid wall. Other ghosts are mischievous in their pranks and tricks when they move things around or close doors to get a little attention from the living.

But is there such a thing as an embarrassed ghost?

Guests at the Roanoke Island Inn on the waterfront in Manteo might very well say so.

The actual ghost, he may not agree, though.

The Roanoke Island Inn sits peacefully on the verdant bank of Shallowbag Bay in Manteo, its windows overlooking the marina and Roanoke Sound to the east. It's an old house, for an old town. Even with its large stately appearance, it seems nestled into the island, like a comfy cat on a rocker. The original building was built sometime after the Civil War in the 1870s by Asa and Martha Jones as a home, long before roads were needed on Roanoke Island. The best access was by water, so it was built just off the waterway where a boat could easily reach the home. Over the years the house has grown. Fernando Street and parking for cars along the reed covered fringe of Shallowbag Bay now front the building, but the old time elegance still graces the inn.

The ghost that haunts it has a quiet elegance all his own.

The Roanoke Island Inn is haunted by a former resident and family member by the name of Roscoe Jones. Roscoe was the son of the original owners, Asa and Martha. Born in 1884, he worked as a postmaster, which was a prestigious and well paying job to have, especially at the young age of twenty five. According to the legend, he was the postmaster for Manteo, which benefited him to be able to step out of his home and almost immediately be at work. He held the position from 1909 until 1915, when he was unceremoniously let go by the US government. Something in the firing shamed the young man. He may have been fired for a specific cause, or just neglect, no one knows. What happened afterwards is what brought about the ghost stories.

Roscoe was retired from his job, and then in his shame chose to retire himself from public life. He went to his room in what is now the Roanoke Island Inn, shut the door, and never came out during the day again. He would only unlock his door and sneak down to the kitchen to eat his dinner, alone, in the darkness of late night, to hide himself from all others. His family would hear him softly treading the stairs or opening doors. Sometimes, if a person was out late at night, they might spy him in shadow on the porch, but no one saw his face again.

The anxiety and shame placed its toll on the man's health, and Roscoe Jones began to wither and die. His body gave up, but it seems his spirit did not.

Soon after Roscoe died, people would spot an ethereal figure in a postman's outfit walking though the inn or leaving the front door. Roscoe was back at his job, trying to fulfill his purpose that had been denied him years before.

Additionally, the sounds of a presence from the afterlife haunt the inn. Footsteps are heard in an empty hall. Items are moved or broken, knocked from tables or shelves. One part of the legend professes of a radio that played music and would not turn off, even when it was unplugged. The appearances of Roscoe Jones as a ghost, and his antics, have been documented and testified for years now. Anyone who has experienced the happenings, be they guests or employees, will swear that the inn is haunted by a mysterious and possibly embarrassed ghost.

But what would Roscoe Jones think about this?

The legend of the Roanoke Island Inn being haunted is well documented. There are too many tales to think this is just one person's imagination. And Roscoe Jones did live, and probably died, in the house. There is just one thing missing from the story.

He died in 1953.

He was sixty eight years old.

In reality, he was not the postmaster of Manteo, but the small town of Griffin, NC. No one has heard of Griffin anymore, even though everyone knows where it is. Griffin was the shortlived name of Nags Head. Many of the towns on the Outer Banks used local or aboriginal names. When the post offices came in, they wanted shorter, easier to say and read names, not strange long names. So there was an attempt to rename Nags Head into Griffin in 1909, the same time that Roscoe Jones got his job as postmaster. The name was changed back sometime around 1915, which coincides with the end of Jones' time as postmaster.

Roscoe Jones probably has nothing to be embarrassed about.

It could be that he just likes his home, and delivering the mail.

The Phantom Fiddler

Hatteras

It was a rare item to have something special and cherished when living on the Cape Hatteras seashore during the 1800s. With little money and no access to the outside world, most of what they had was either made or found. To have a unique handcrafted tool was something seldom seen on the sparse shores. Hezekiah "Carr" Farrow was fortunate indeed to have such an item in his hands. He owned, and played, a beautiful fiddle. The rest of island felt fortunate that they had someone as wonderful as Carr Farrow to play for them.

Well, almost all of the island felt that way.

Parties in the 1800s were community affairs, and everyone brought what they could to share for the events.

The village of Trent, now Frisco, was tight knit. It was difficult to hide one's personal business in a tiny village of only 800 residents. Families and friends would have get-togethers to share good news, good fortune, or to welcome back loved ones from travels and travails. They would always call on Carr to come play his fiddle and kick out a good dance for them. His playing was exquisite, unlike any music ever heard. His fiddle could play a lively reel or a slow ballad in time and tune to the mood needed.

Carr's fiddle was a fine instrument. He would prepare it lovingly. As with all the items they used, Carr had to make much of what he needed. He would stretch and dry his own strings from cattle gut, and bind his own bow with horse hair. His fiddle was his only way of earning a living, so he cherished the instrument like a parent protects a child.

One day he was asked to play for a wedding of a young woman, Angeline, who was marrying her beloved boyfriend who had been away for months working a fishing boat in the Caribbean to raise money for his future married life. With the man returning from a long voyage, the celebration had to be extensive, so only the best would do. Food was prepared by the family and friends, and even a local delicacy, yaupon tea, a dark and bitter hot drink that was both prized and addictive to some locals, was boiled up. The tannins were so strong that they often turned the teeth black on people who partook in the drink. Locals would choose not to smile rather than give away their secret drink to outsiders. But among friends, when Carr Farrow was coming to play, everyone smiled.

On his way walking to the house, Carr was passed by a cousin. His cousin asked, "Where are you off to?"

"I'm off to play fiddle at Miss Angeline's wedding ceremony and reception," explained Carr.

His cousin, also a fiddle player, had hoped to be come as popular as Carr was. He desired to play farther up the beach, in Kinnakeet, where there were more houses and potentially more money. He asked with a gleam in his eye on the case that held Carr's beautiful fiddle, "How about you let me go play that fiddle over at Miss Angeline's party tonight? I sure would love to make that beautiful thing sing."

Carr smiled a tight lipped smile to his envious cousin, "No, cos, I think I will play this fiddle tonight. And tomorrow night. And every night I feel like it until the night I die." He planted his feet in the sandy road as if to affirm his words. "But you just keep walking to Kinnakeet with your own fiddle. I'm sure you will make it there sometime!"

Carr waited for his cousin to move on, then hustled his way to the home of Angeline and her family where they gathered for the wedding.

The dance started with a kiss, and kept going from there. Carr Farrow played with his heart, and everyone felt the lively tunes come. So lively was the music, and so jovial were the revelers, that no one, not even Carr Farrow himself, noticed any change in the tunes. His lightheadedness was surely from the heat and playing so hard. The ache in his arm was only from how much he worked his bow. The pounding in his heart was just the love and joy he felt for the music he made.

No one noticed anything amiss until the music stopped and poor Carr Farrow fell dead on the spot.

The revelers immediately became mourners. They had all seen death before. They knew there was nothing to be done for the man. They did their best to carry his mortal remains back to his family home. Carr's father said he rested easier knowing that his son had died doing what he loved. Carr's visage was one of peaceful happiness, eyes closed and a wide smile showing dark stained teeth.

A body won't last long on the beach. Cold winds or sunny days made little difference. So a hasty wake was prepared for the villagers to say goodbye, as Carr was displayed in a simple casket, dressed in his finest clothes, and his beloved fiddle lay next to him. His cousin spoke to Carr's father, "Uncle, I know how much he loved that fiddle, but it seems a waste to bury it and never let it be heard again."

With that thought, Carr's father gave the fiddle to the cousin. And when the cousin played, the sound was a beautiful melancholy tune that befitted both the solemn occasion and the instrument well.

For weeks he would play the fiddle, and people swore it sounded just as good as if Carr himself held the bow. The cousin enjoyed playing a fine instrument instead of the cheaper cat scratching sound of his old fiddle. With his skill, he soon was asked to play his first wedding. But when he went to get "his" fiddle, he discovered the case to be light, too light to have anything in it.

Cursing his luck, "Stolen!" he cried, "No doubt some sailor has it all the way to a port in Virginia or to be lost in a rum soaked shack in the tropics soon enough!"

The cousin took his original fiddle, but the tune he played came off sour and scratchy. The crowd found no life or joy in the music, and left early. He knew this would be the beginning and end to his performances, and the cousin sulked away into Trent Woods, down Flower Ridge Road, his old violin case in his hand.

The winds blew late and cold, with the March sunset blotted out by the gray. It was a bad day made miserable by the weather, and the wind whistled in the still bare trees. Then, he noticed that it wasn't the wind whistling. It was a musical rhythm. It was a fiddle playing a sorrowful ballad, in time with his own footsteps. Only it continued as he stopped on the dirt road to listen.

And look.

He recognized the sound as his fiddle. Or, he realized, Carr's fiddle. For there he was, in the wind blown path of Flower Ridge Road, directly across from the grave of Hezekiah "Carr" Farrow.

He dropped his case and ran, never stopping until he slammed his own door shut to his back.

Carr Farrow died at the young age of fifty years old, in 1858. He was buried in his family's small cemetery on Flower Ridge Road, a shady path that has been long guarded by the ever circling light of Cape Hatteras Lighthouse. And from the day that his cousin first heard the sounds, people have heard the unearthly music of Carr's fiddle in the trees along the road. Kids would avoid the spot in fear when the days crossed into evenings. The path may have been a shortcut to their homes, but it was hardly worth it to have to pass the spooky grave and its music. Locals will testify to the events. When outsiders say "It's probably just the wind in the trees," the natives shake their heads and whistle a mournful tune. They know the difference between the unpitched cry of wind in the branches and the song of a fiddle player, long passed but still performing. It is a wordless song, reminding people of the regrets of covetousness and envy from events long ago. Cherish what you have but take nothing that is not truly yours.

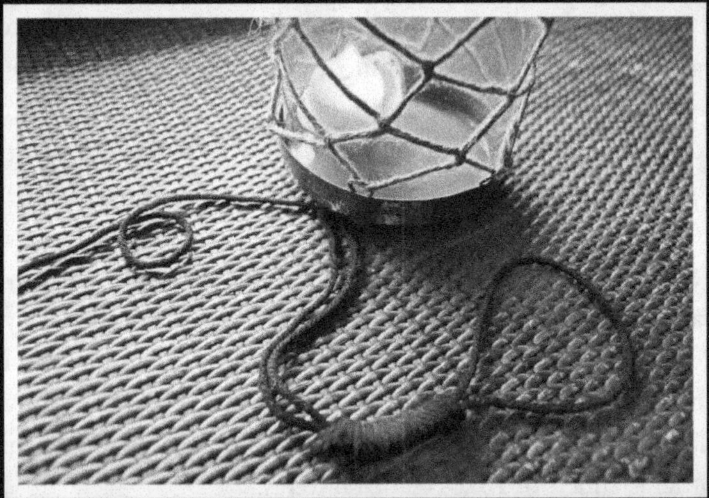

Spinning the Witch's Wheel

Frisco

Taking a look at the legends that are buried deep within the history of the Outer Banks, one would think that witchcraft and sorcery was the most popular occupation along the coast, especially for single women. Possibly the only pastime more popular was accusing women of being witches. That action made life difficult and often short for the women so accused, but for the people that were confident in their accusations, it never ended well for them, either.

Polly Poiner was a witch.

At least, that's what everyone said.

All of the locals of Trent Woods, the land that would become Frisco on Hatteras Island in later years, were sure of this. Her actions were the very definition of witchcraft. The little old lady, all alone in her small home, was known to cackle and hoot. Her mocking and teasing taunt whenever someone tried to confront her or accuse her was enough to scare most people off. She had a skill with herbs and plants that bordered on potion making. And she was known for her constant spinning of her spinning wheel, where she took gathered wool to make her yarn. The picture of an old lady, cackling deviously, as she spun and spun compulsively, continually making her yarn until she finally ran out of wool, the windows of her shack frosted by salt and lit by the yellow flame of an oil lamp, would define the image of a witch to the other islanders of 1820s Cape Hatteras.

Now, most people would know to leave a witch alone. They don't take chances with someone who would cast a spell over them. Absolum Scarborough was not one of those people. He couldn't stand the woman. Her mocking cackles made the hair on the back of his neck rise. His sheep would go missing and she would spin her wool. Then his cattle began dying, as well.

It drove the man mad.

Sure that Polly was a witch, and sure that she was the cause of his misfortune, he felt his fury flame deep inside him. He decided to end Polly Poiner's life.

When his last head of cattle died, he broke into Polly's home and strangled her to death as she sat at her spinning wheel.

Sure that he had solved his problem, as well as the problem of many others, he left Polly's lifeless body in her home, hoping that was the end of everything.

It was the end for him, even if not at that exact moment. It became the beginning of a long and terrifying haunting for the rest of the island in later years.

Back then, Hatteras was part of Hyde County, which was on the mainland west side of the Outer Banks. Scarborough was hauled up to a jury trial for the crime of murder. Everyone knew he had done it, for he had even bragged and boasted that one day he would kill her if she pushed him too far. Scarborough knew well enough not to completely admit his crime, so he only hinted at what he had done. He claimed, "I didn't kill her, but if I believed she was a witch, I woulda killed her like I kill a snake!" His sideways claim to the judge and jury that he was doing a service by ridding the island of a witch, while not actually acknowledging he killed her, didn't go as he had planned. He was found guilty and sentenced to hang by the neck until dead. He met the end of his life at the end of a rope at the old Lake Landing Courthouse in Hyde County in 1826.

Scarborough had put in an argument to the case, asking the judgement to be thrown out. Three of the six members of the jury that had found him guilty were related to Poiner. The petition actually was approved, but the notice from Raleigh made it to Hyde County three days after Scarborough was hanged.

With both Poiner and Scarborough dead and gone, one would think that there would be an end to the nasty business.

But Poiner had other plans. For a time, Scarborough's land was left fallow, but the need to grow food and use the land for grazing was great. Soon enough, others tried to plow the land. No seed would take harvest, no plant would grow, and no animal would graze upon even the scraps of weed that dared to take hold there.

More mysteriously, when the ground was cut with a plow, the soil would loosen to a soft dust. The sand would swirl and spin, like the wheel of a spinning wheel. At night, where Poiner's house had stood, people would see her, still spinning maniacally, constantly making yarn. And through the darkness they heard her cackle, her laugh. When the soil was overturned, a mysterious rope would appear, like a snake, to chase the plow, plowman, and beast. Then it would form itself in the shape of a giant noose, all the while spinning and swirling, constantly circling.

Polly Poiner couldn't escape the crazed wrath of Absolum Scarborough, but she found a way to avenge her death. Poiner remained there as a ghost to be a reminder that no one should blame another, especially a little old woman who lives by herself, for their own bad fortune. Was she really a witch, or just a solitary woman who didn't want some irritating man pushing her around, making up stories about her? Or did Scarborough create his own curse when he murdered Poiner, bringing about his own demise at the end of a short rope on a pole by the water?

Ghost Lights Of The Outer Banks

Nags Head

A ship's captain, facing a determined sea with a will to twist his sailing craft to splinters, has the perilous position of risking his fate to the ocean or hoping against hope to find shelter in a harbor somewhere along the barren North Carolina coast in the dark of night. His ship has a bone in its mouth, as the north winds drive waves onto the bow, making it foam with white and green bioluminescence. But the craft makes little headway against the determined sea. The wind roars. The ship bobs. The crew cowers. The captain stews. He has little in the way of options.

Suddenly, good fortune shines upon him. To port, he sees a bobbing light. It rolls slowly up and down, a decidedly calm movement compared to the pitching his deck is currently doing. He orders a turn, head for the light. There is a ship in the harbor there. There is safety. There is companionship. There he will ride out the storm until daybreak, and make safer passage to the cities up north where he can unload and recover from this treacherous voyage.

Little does the captain know, there is no ship. There is no safe haven. Only a shallow sandbar awaits him and his ship. The hidden shallows are ready to reach up and break his keel, send his masts falling, and crush his crew. He will be stranded until the locals, land pirates all of them, will row out to strip the broken vessel bare of its supplies. And then the crew will be sent to a murderous and cold blooded end. There will be no one left to tell the tale. No warning will be passed on to the next ship passing by.

And the light he saw, the last light he would see in his life, would stumble back to its stable. A horse, an old and broken down nag with a feeble oil light tied under its neck, was walked across the rolling dunes to mimic the sight of a ship safe in a harbor. It would lure in unsuspecting ships for the local pirates living in the shadow of Jockey's Ridge to pillage.

It would be the cause for the land and the town to earn its name, Nags Head, for the poor broken nag with a lamp tied under its head.

The stories would be passed on to become myth and legend, with bits and pieces tied together in a not so neat bundle. The tale of how Nags Head got its name would be told and retold, people would believe the stories, and myth turned into truth, all the while selling a million toy horses with lamps on their necks in the process.

What some have come to realize is that part of the legend isn't really true.

A horse would not tolerate a lamp around their neck, with a candle slowly burning away just under their throat. Nor would a horse walking along the seashore dunes or Jockey's Ridge create the placid effect of a ship bobbing at anchor in a safe harbor. The name Nags Head is an old name. Likely the land was named after one of the several places in Great Britain that share the moniker. An early landowner probably noticed the similarity to a coast in England, and simply gave it the same name. It is a rather ho-hum realization to an otherwise exciting tale.

What most don't think about afterwards is this...

Where were the lights coming from?

Today, with all the modern houses built up on the Outer Banks, the old dunes are either gone or barely visible. Only Jockey's Ridge has been well preserved as a park. Most other dunes that existed in the hundreds of years before have been torn down, covered, or simply sit unseen and unnoticed on an increasingly unnatural Outer Banks.

But they used to be here.

And they used to have lights.

The ghost lights of the Outer Banks were a rather common and even accepted event up into the 1970s. Before the great swath of development first hit the beaches, one could look from sea to sound and find a dune line across the western side of the islands.

In Nags Head, south of Jockey's Ridge, there once stood the Seven Sisters. They were so named because of the tale that surrounded their creation. Seven sisters, by blood or just by promise, freed themselves from slavery of an owner of a beach cottage and left, walking in a row, the very moment they found their freedom. They disappeared as they walked from the beach to the sound. The next night, a terrible storm blew in, and in the morning, seven dunes stood, in a staggered row, marching away to freedom.

Jockey's Ridge once was three sets of dunes, each building on the other as a place for matchmaking. The smallest dune to the north was Courtship Hill, followed by Engagement Hill, and finally Wedding Hill, where a small church once stood nearby.

In Kill Devil Hills still stands Run Hill, which protects the peaceful sanctuary of Nags Head Woods, along with all the ghosts that reside in there, from the cold bitter salt winds of the north.

Up to Kitty Hawk there still exists a series of low rolling dunes. Once they were the home to the Wright Brothers and their tent while they experimented with kites and gliders. Now they are covered with homes and roads, but underneath, the dunes still roll.

Even far up north, past Corolla, into what used to be the true wilds of the Outer Banks, stands Penny's Hill, a great marker beacon of sand that is the most visible of a long chain of dunes that slowly rolled over the small towns that once dotted the Currituck coast.

At one time, strange ghost lights appeared over all these dunes.

The Seven Sisters light was predictable, almost common. It could be seen most evenings as families drove by the dunes. A bright white light, brighter than any flashlight or headlight, would hover just above the dunes, as if a star was balanced on a string just above the ridge. Parents driving by would point it out, "Look, there's the ghost light," as if it were merely mundane. Kids would get excited and follow the light as they passed by. No matter how many times they looked, it always appeared to be just over the dune. It was not an optical illusion or trick of a light coming from far off Manteo. The ghost light of the Seven Sisters hovered over the dunes, real as can be, as assured in its existence as it was mysterious in its cause. Sadly, the light and the dunes disappeared in the 1980s when the Seven Sisters were plowed under for a mall.

Run Hill was once easily visible from throughout Kill Devil Hills. It stuck up high over the sound, just south of the Wright Brothers Memorial. A strange red light would appear in the evening that could be seen for miles, even as far as the beach. As the sun set, the light stayed in the same place until the sky darkened. Then the red light would slowly fade to nothingness, making the viewer wonder if it was ever there at all. Then it would do the same thing again, week after week.

The most famous of these lights is of course the light seen at Jockey's Ridge. The legends tell of it softly bobbing like a ship in a harbor, but that is likely more due to the viewer than the light. The light became so prevalent that the legends grew up around it. Land pirates and the suffering nag leading a lamp on its neck attached themselves to the name, but the light was there long before there was a Nags Head.

So what are the lights, and where are they now? Sadly, the lights are all but gone now. The lights never appeared around people, and with Jockey's Ridge a popular vacation spot for sunsets, the light has not appeared for decades. The Seven Sisters fell to the bulldozer, and Run Hill now abuts the local school and housing developments.

The lights no longer shine. What they were is unknown, and with them no longer appearing, we may never know the cause. Ghost lights are mysterious forces of nature. North Carolina is full of them, from Maco Light on the coast to Brown Mountain Lights up along the Blue Ridge Parkway. They simply are that they are, acts of nature that remind us that there is more to our world than we can perceive with our own senses. The lights will go down in history as a true unknown, a mystery that will never be solved.

The Ghost Of The Water Fire
Nags Head

The O'Cockers call it "water fire." Kayakers refer to it as "sea sparkle." Scientists call it bioluminescence. When the tiny plankton get well fed on summer heat, and the tropical winds blow out of the southeast, these microscopic creatures get blown out of the Caribbean and whipped into the Gulf Stream. The rare occurrence will light up the shores along the Outer Banks in late summer and fall, turning the ocean waves an electric blue or glowing green. The waves churn and crash, filled with the little sea sparkles, exciting them into giving off the strange ghostly light. It is best seen on cloudy nights, without the moon to brighten the view.

Water fire is an uncommon occurrence. It is unpredictable, turbulent, and almost finicky in where it appears. But there is another sight, just as rare, and definitely even more strange and undefinable.

When the ocean lights up, on dark, moonless nights, and the waves glow blue and green from the plankton, a lucky few have seen him.

A phantom surfer, the ghost of the water fire.

Only on the darkest of nights will you see him. The waves must curve into clean barrels or roll from the offshore sandbars. They have to be good. No chop or close out swell will do. The description that the few people who have seen him are all similar.

They sit on the beach, watching the glowing waves, mesmerized by the glow. Each wave is the same, but still unique. The water lights up as the waves pack themselves tightly as they plan their rush to the beach. The crest of the wave glows, and then brightens as it churns over like a waterfall in a long procession up the beach. The whole front of the wave shines.

Then they see him. He is noticed first by the darker shape on the glowing nighttime waves. He is an ethereal figure, black and gray and misty, cut through by the salt spray of the shore break. He slowly forms into a human figure, a dark shape riding a black surf board. Behind him, as the wave breaks into a tube or closes out, a bright trail of the plankton leave a streaking comet through the water. They are turned on by the wake and fins of the phantom surfboard.

He usually is described riding a longer board, and doesn't prefer to do the usual shreds of young riders. He glides, softly, confidently, with little motion other than wandering up and down the board. When the wave finally gives up its power, as it gets closer to shore, the surfer is seen slowing down to kick his board up and over the wave. But as he makes that last crest, he vanishes into a salty black mist.

Then he appears again, where he started. No one sees him paddle out. No one has seen him come ashore. He just rides the glowing waves with calm comfort and efficiency.

The ghost surfer will ride as long as the waves are good, and the water glows. No one has ever seen him long enough to know how long he will surf. Since he only appears when the plankton appear, the apparition is rarely seen. He has surfed more than one break, but seems to prefer being in the dark just out of the lights of the Nags Head Fishing Pier. He has also surfed just south of Martin Street in Kill Devil Hills.

No one is really sure who the ghost surfer is. Some stories say he was a young doctor who died in the 1990s when he drowned saving a boy washed into the ocean on a cold March day. The doctor was a surfer who preferred going out in the evenings after his work was done, and the beaches were empty of tourists and swimmers. Instead of appearing only on the anniversary of his death, he only shows up when the waves are good, which would make sense for a surfer, be him ghost or living.

Others tie the apparition in to popular locals who have passed on that were once part of the surf scene, or a history from long ago, when surfing was in its infancy in the 50s and

60s. He may be a manifestation of the coast itself, honoring and remembering those who rode the waves and cared about the shore for so long.

We may never know who the Ghost Surfer is. Those who see him are in a very rare and exclusive club as witnesses to the paranormal. But he is in a club by himself. While we may be fortunate to see the ghost surfer out on the glowing waves in the dark of night, he is the only one who truly gets to experience the ride of eternity, a truly endless ride of joy and contentment, where the summer winds blow, the ocean is warm, and the waves light his way.

The Mystery Of The Haunted House
Kill Devil Hills

"It sounded a lot like the title of an old Nancy Drew book," thought Stephanie Benchley as she drove past the large beachfront lot of half constructed houses. It was the first time she had been home to the Outer Banks in a year. The old blue and white beach house, with the gazebo out front and the old carriage house garage had always been there. Always. Since her family had moved down to Kill Devil Hills, before she was born. She always remembered the "haunted house." It was a landmark. One that she was sure would somehow stand forever, holding the ghostly secrets that every little kid on the Outer Banks wanted to crack open, but were too terrified to try.

Stephanie thought back to her attempt to see who or what was in that creepy old house.

It was 1983, and she was a precocious tomboy of twelve, going on twenty, her daddy always said. Her family owned a beach house down the beach road only a few blocks. It was drafty, hot in the summer, leaky, smelling of salt and driftwood, like any true beach house should, she remembered. Every time they drove up the beach road, her father would point with one finger at the old place, where there was never a car, never a visitor, and say, "There's the Haunted House!"

And she knew it was haunted. Everyone knew. The place looked spooky, even in the daylight. It was always in this state of arrested decay, with Joe Bells growing through the cracks of the old tabby driveway and peeling paint on the sides. It never got worse looking. It never got better, either. When she was a little kid, she asked her father why it was haunted. He explained, "I think people just say that because it's old and empty."

But no one believed that. Her father was just trying to placate her fears. That place was haunted. Haunted as can be. Seeing it in the daylight made you *think* it was haunted. Seeing it at night, you *knew* it was.

At night, whenever they passed it, little lights flickered in the windows. The glass was old, maybe as old as the house, and that was old. Again, her father attributed the flickering to car headlights. Stephanie knew there had to be more.

Her friends knew all the legends. If they didn't know, then the parents did. The old families, the true Outer Bankers, the "Hoi Toiders" that sold her family fish and shrimp, they had been told by their parents, and the stories got passed down, right to Stephanie and the other kids her age.

She remembered Brody Wright, a sweaty, annoying kid a year older than her once told the entire Sunday School class at her church about how a girl that lived there fell down a well and died, and her ghost still haunts the house. Joe Beasley had later squashed that rumor with great effect. He and Stephanie stood on the banks of Colington Creek, chucking rocks into the water. He "aw shucks"ed that story with a great heave, sending a rock all the way into far off Kitty Hawk Bay for emphasis. "Naow," she said with his drawl, "It was a boy that died there. He pestered his mom around the house until she told him to go play in the ocean and leave her alone. He went out and drownded."

Either story was good enough for Stephanie. Either one meant the place was haunted. Boy or girl, well or ocean, there was definitely something haunting that old house.

One story that everyone knew, everyone older than her, at least, was this. After the tragedy, the parents up and left the house, never to return. They left it just the way it was that day. People said they peered into the windows, covered with salt, and could still see the furniture inside. Plates on the table, old toys along the fireplace and mantle. And they would testify to a feeling of foreboding or an ill wind. "Something is definitely there," they would always say.

Stephanie thought it curious that every story she heard about the place, after the cause of the haunting, was always the same. "These kids are just repeating what they've heard," she told herself. "They never went to that place. Not on their own."

And she would have been right. For all the bluster that the twelve year old boys had, none of them had a car, and there was no way their moms were going to let them ride a bike out at night from the sound side homes to a haunted house all by themselves, at night.

But Stephanie was twelve going on twenty. She had a beach house just a half mile down the road from the haunted house. Her family was going to stay there, just for fun, over the Easter holidays, so they could get it ready for summer. They normally lived on the sound side, like most locals, where they were sheltered from the cold winds of winter, and isolated from the tourists of summer. But they would go over to their little cottage on the beach and enjoy a bit of springtime peace.

Her parents were going out on a date one night. She had long ago proven she was quite capable of taking care of herself, and at twelve, going on twenty, certainly didn't need a babysitter. So Stephanie hatched a plan to investigate the haunted house.

She waited until after 6:00 to walk out. It needed to be dark when she got there, she thought to herself, but she wasn't going to walk down the beach in complete darkness. She was going alone, and she didn't need to fool anyone into thinking she wasn't scared, because she was a little. Admitting that in her own head steeled her resolve. She was proving nothing to no one, except to herself.

As she walked down the beach, the last light of a sunset the color of lipstick painted the April evening sky. The shadows of the dunes had already crept over the sand. Stars were just trying to twinkle out over the ocean, and far off on the horizon a bright green light appeared on a freighter headed south. A few lights burned in houses along the shore, but most stood dark and empty, silhouetted against the sunset in their black on black suits. She could see the bright flaring lights of Avalon Fishing Pier burning out over the ocean. With no one out on the beach, it was a peaceful, but eerie, feeling that came over her.

She reviewed what little she learned about the house. Outside of the legend that it was haunted, and no one ever seemed to stay there, she didn't know much more. The house was built sometime between 1890 and 1930. That didn't help any. It only made things more vague for her. And she was pretty sure that the little girl falling in a well was made up after a baby died tragically at another family home nearby. So, no ghosts in a well, that was good, at least.

She had almost convinced herself that the place maybe wasn't haunted when she got there, and began to stealthily walk up the sandy path to the old haunted house. "The old haunted house," she even said it out loud. "Just when I think it's not haunted, I go and call it that."

It was fully dark by the time she made it to the house. The Wright Brothers Monument just started to shine with its green spotlights on the big pylon. But where Stephanie stood, she and the house were one in darkness. The long, long walkway, straight as an arrow and nowhere to hide, led up to the back porch. Her footsteps clomped loudly on the old wood with every step, even as she walked barefoot over the bridge. She stopped to slip on her tennis shoes, out of fear of splinters, and of making enough noise to wake the ghosts. She didn't even consider that a human might be home. No light came from the back.

Stephanie worried as she crossed the open walkway. "Would someone see me," she wondered, "and call the police?" She knew she was trespassing, but so many people were curious about the place, surely others had done this before. She was fairly relieved when she got to the darkness of the back porch.

That relief was short lived as she stood in the pitch black. She hadn't bothered to bring a flashlight and she could see nothing. No lights on the inside, no light outside. Then she felt her skin crawl. "Someone stepped on my grave," she thought seriously. The expression added to her shivers. A feeling of dread and cold came over her. It was more than her own fear, or the feeling that she shouldn't be there. It was as if something didn't want her there. She backed up out of the shadows involuntarily, like she had been politely but firmly shoved.

Stephanie suddenly felt like she needed some light. She walked quickly around the house. She tried to stay in shadows, but also find some light to her way. The house seemed to lean on her, or was it her pressing against the house? She couldn't tell. Walking past the old garage, with its wooden doors built more for horse drawn carriages than modern cars, she heard a strange clicking from inside. It stopped when she stopped, started when she walked. It was a disturbingly rhythmic cricket or mouse in there that followed Stephanie as she walked alongside the house.

No car passed, so she walked out to the gazebo. The floor was warped and rotten, so she didn't dare stand on it. Instead, she hid behind it, sheltering there, hidden from any potential passing car, but still able to see the house from the front. The view in the failing light was no better than the darkness of the back. In fact, thought Stephanie, it was probably worse. Now she could see how scary it was. She still felt that feeling of dread.

A car passed slowly down the beach road. Stephanie saw how the headlights reflected haphazardly in the old glass. It was warped, wavy, and brown. The light seemed to be trapped in the glass, swimming around from pane to pane for too long a time as the car drove by. The reflections stayed far too long after the car had passed.

Again alone, Stephanie screwed up her courage. She had come this far. She strode up to the windows on the front of the house to look in. There was no light, no one was home, obviously, but there were no lamps on to illuminate the insides. She saw nothing. Walking up on the porch, she crouched behind the old wooden railing. She hoped her figure would be obscured in the wavy shadows of the porch rails as she looked through the old windows and door.

Cars drove by on the far distant bypass, but the light barely made it to the glass. She waited for a car to pass by so she could look in with some clarity. Finally, an old truck drove down the road, its engine roaring ineffectually compared to its low speed.

Stephanie was finally able to glance inside as the headlights swept across the windows. She saw inside for a moment. It was exactly as people had said. The house was a time capsule. Old wooden furniture sat neatly across the living room. A brick fireplace with a dark maw of a hearth, no fire, no life, was up against one wall. She imagined she saw toys on the mantle, but they could have been old seashells, the way her imagination was running at the moment.

The one thing that she did see clearly was a small rocking chair, near the window. Small and meant for a child.

She was half sure she saw it moving.

Then she was positive it was just a trick of the light, as the truck's headlights skirted across the front of the house.

Then she wondered if she was right the first time.

Stephanie thought, "I'll wait for one more car to come by, and look in again. Just to see if the rocking chair is moving. Then I'll go home." She was scared now. This time two parts of her mind argued. One knew she was frightened by what she might see. The other tried to convince her that she really wasn't scared. Stephanie wondered who would win in an argument with herself.

When no car came by in the next thirty seconds, fear started to get ahead. She wasn't sure if the voice that was saying "Go away" was in her head or in the house. With her last bit of determination, she walked quickly down the steps without looking back. She walked around the south side of the house. She was going to avoid the strange sounds from the garage if she could help it. "If I can keep this all normal," she told herself, "I can get to the beach before something comes out and gets me."

Instead of going up onto the back porch, in the pitch dark, she tromped through the sharp sticky reeds and sea oats that scratched at her jeans and promised to poke her with every step. Stephanie heaved herself up the little wooden walkway and began to walk back to the beach.

With her last bit of courage, now that she was far enough away, she turned around to look one more time. She saw through the windows the same strange orange light of headlamps flickering across the old glass. It looked like the way old hurricane lamps put out their yellow fire through salt coated glass.

Then she looked to see where the car's headlights were coming from.

No cars passed the old haunted house.

She saw the lights inside, still flickering.

Inside a house that she knew to be empty, empty, empty...

Stephanie shook the old memories from her head as she drove into the driveway of her own beach house. It was bright and cared for, all yellow and green and gray paint, with life inside and out. Her daughter had left her boogie board out front, and her husband had towels draped over the railings. It was all new and full of the beach for an old house.

Stephanie never told anyone of her secret journey to the old haunted house. When she was younger, she worried she would get in trouble, and when she got older, she realized that her story did nothing to explain the old legends. She didn't even know what it had meant to her. She just knew the place was haunted.

The haunted house became haunted by age and rot, with no care for the house itself, nor the spirits inside. Stephanie would see it fall to the bulldozer within a month of returning home, and whatever ghosts were in there were lost to time. Stephanie wondered if the new houses to be built there would ever see any of the sights she saw, or know the legends that the locals told. Would the stories die when the house died?

Perhaps it was time to tell someone, she thought as her daughter came running out of the house to see her.

Afterword

At the beginning of this book, I mentioned how these were ghost stories, with emphasis on *stories*. I was describing how they are fun to tell. They are entertaining and scary. Stories take the reader somewhere. It takes a little time to get there, and we enjoy the feeling of the ride when we read a story. That's what they are supposed to do.

Here, I will again emphasize *stories*. But in a different way. Ghost tales are works of fiction by nature, with a bit of history or legend or fact tied in for good measure. This is not to say they are not real. Nor are they made up. All the tales in this book have been told or passed down from one to another in some form. Most of the events and places are real. These things really did happen.

There just is a little bit of license that storytellers take to make a ghost tale that little bit better. The spider droops down from its web slowly; it doesn't just fall on your shoulder. You have to set the mood with a ghost story. You tell it and embellish it, just a touch.

When I wrote *Did You See That Ghost?*, I added a section at the end that was called "The Rest Of The Tale", where I explained some of the realities of the ghost stories and legends. I didn't want to ruin them in the book by telling readers that the stories were just urban legends. I also added some facts that made the stories all the more real, but didn't fit in with the general feel of the chapter.

When writing this book, I felt like I should do the same thing. Some of the facts and history of these legends may be important, but also a little dry or historical. I didn't want to ruin the spooky feel. However, they do have some value to the legends themselves.

It was harder to find the stories in this book than in ones past because they were hidden a little deeper. They weren't shared often, either in oral tradition or written down. Because of that, the history and facts have gotten blurred over. I think that's too bad, because all that is still important.

Two of the stories in here happened to me. The story of the graves in Nags Head Woods and the old Haunted House are my stories.

I really did tickle a tree and have it start to shake. There are quite a few old tiny cemeteries hidden and overgrown in Nags head Woods. All of the older houses are now long gone, but a few stone foundations still remain. Nags Head Woods was actually a populated village in more recent times, up until the 1950s, with some small fishing shacks still remaining much later on. Most of these places have become overgrown and hidden now. It is managed as a nature preserve. The care for the area is now done to maintain trail access to the natural land.

And I did go over to the old Haunted House and see weird lights flickering when there were no lights around. The Haunted House is an old, old legend that was held very close to us locals from long ago. It was old when I was young, and the legend was vague even then. Depending upon who is asked, the place was haunted by a girl that downed in a well or a boy that drowned in the surf. The parents always left in distress, never to return. The house was said to be left in a state of arrest, with the child's toys still around the house, and the room preserved as a shrine. Even the age of the house is unknown, with some evidence of it being built in 1930, others saying a much earlier date of 1890, with updates done decades later. The child's death is probably apocryphal. A baby girl did die, not from falling in a well, but from more natural causes, at another family home nearby, which may be the origin of the legend. The Haunted House was really just considered haunted because it was old and creepy, and no one was ever seen in it. Sadly, the house was torn down for a new development.

The tales of the Phantom Surfer and the lights on the Seven Sisters and Run Hill dunes are also real events. They have very little history to them. The lights on the dunes were so common, we would see them all the time. Even as a little kid, I had no issues with wandering out alone or with my neighborhood friends out to the dunes near my house. I would often wonder why we didn't just go out to see what the light was. It is strange to look back and see how such a mysterious set of events could be so commonplace, so accepted as real, that no one bothered to even walk out and see what was happening. Who knows, maybe someone did, and no one believed them when they got back. Again, it's a set of legends that will never have an answer.

Some of the other chapters were much more difficult to figure out. Finding these stories took a bit more digging. I knew the tales from when I was a kid, but again, it was just a short mention. The story of the phantom hand was only a snippet of a tale I knew from the 1970s. The history and events, like the big granite block sliding off a barge, which I have seen in the shallow water near my childhood home, are all true. The doors closed on the monument were always told to us to be locked because someone had a terrible panic attack after being stuck on the stairs going up the inside of the monument. Other stories I had to shorten to make the tale worth telling. The story of Polly Poiner, that one is real, right up to the hauntings. I have heard people say the land of Trent Woods, near the Cape Hatteras Lighthouse, is haunted by her. I just don't know if it really is. I do know that her story is real. In reality, a man named Absolum Scarborough killed May Midyeht, and claimed as his defense that she was a witch who sunk his boat. Her name is interesting to see, as it shows how the surnames of some Outer Bankers change over time, with that Midyeht becoming the more common Midgett and Midgette. But that doesn't help a ghost story.

Stories like the wedding ring, the ghostly woman walking the road around Hatteras, and the Hatteras fiddler are all chestnuts. They have been told locally, as well as experienced by the same locals, for years. They just haven't been well preserved in written form. The versions in this book took a bit of artistic license to make the tales entertaining. But every version I have heard through the years were just as different. We have been putting our own voice to these ghost stories for decades.

And obviously, some of the works here are if not works of fiction, at least fictionalized tales. Buffalo City certainly had its share of ghosts during Prohibition, but who knows what really goes on there now. And while the story of the *Nuova Ottavia* shipwreck is told through the eyes of a fictional character, and his fictional dog, it is a pretty accurate description of a very sad event that still reverberates with the haunted sounds of the past coming through into today.

I think my favorite part of learning about all these legends was how the legends lead to real hard history. Like learning that Nags Head was once for a short time called Griffin, Roscoe Jones really was the postmaster for the town. Whether he haunts the Roanoke Island Inn, I will leave up to you. But the little bit of history I liked most was that the Wright Brothers really did note that they had heard of Miss Mabe, the witch of Nags Head Woods. I can only imagine what it was like for two engineers like the Wrights, dedicated to studying their science, to come to this coast and learn that there was a woman who was successfully practicing witchcraft, powerful enough to change the winds, and that the local residents readily acquiesced to her power.

So, these are the stories. These are the ones I heard. They are the stories I told. I have repeated them here, with some embellishment, some mysterious spice to the local chowder that is the Outer Banks. Not everyone will know these tales. Some will remember them differently. That's fine with me. Tell them differently. I'm not going to say you are wrong. I just hope you can give me a little chill. That's the goal of a good ghost story.

About the Author

Joe Sledge is the author of four books in the Did You See That? series, a collection of roadside attractions across North Carolina, with the coordinates of each location included. Joe has also written two other books of ghost tales besides this book, *Haunting The Outer Banks, Thirteen Tales Of Terror From The North Carolina Coast* and *In The Shadows Of The Pines, Thirteen Mysterious Tales From The Old North State.* Additionally, Joe penned two works of fiction. *Bess Truly And Her Zap-Gun Rangers* is a book written for his daughter which is equal parts Nancy Drew and Radar Men From The Moon. Under the pen name John Martell, Joe wrote *The Unmerciful Sea,* a horror novel that takes place in Ocracoke. He also edited and annotated *Nag's Head; Or, Two Months Among The Bankers,* first written in 1850 about vacation life on the Outer Banks.

Joe is a graduate of UNC Chapel Hill and an avid traveler. When not writing, he and his family spend as much time as possible traveling throughout North Carolina and beyond. In addition to writing, Joe runs Gravity Well Books, his publishing company.

Photo Credits

All photos by Joe Sledge, unless otherwise noted. All photos are under copyright of their owner(s), and are used with permission. Copyright of photos is extended from the initial copyright at the beginning of this book. No duplication or use is allowed without consent of the owners of the photos. Photos are used for entertainment purposes only, and may not be the actual location of the tale.